NEW YORK CITY.
WE WERE KEEPING TABS ON AN OLD MAN WITH A BIG MOUTH.

HI. MY NAME IS CHRIS AND I'M AN ALCOHOLIC.

SPILLING HIS GUTS AT HIS ALCOHOLICS ANONYMOUS MEETINGS, DIVULGING EXTREMELY SENSITIVE GOVERNMENT SECRETS. HE WAS A TICKING PARANORMAL TIME BOMB.

IT'S BEEN THREE DAYS SINCE MY LAST DRINK. I **WAS** SOBER GOIN' ON TEN YEARS.
BUT I WAS TALKING TO AN OLD FRIEND FROM THE SERVICE AND I... FELL OFF THE WAGON AND I FEEL LIKE I JUST NEED TO GET THIS OFF MY CHEST.

ACCORDING TO THE BOSSES, "THE ANIMAL" CHRIS DODGE'S UNSTABLE BEHAVIOR MADE HIM A LIABILITY. WE WERE THERE TO CONFIRM.
'MEMBER THAT THING ABOUT THE WMD'S IN IRAQ? THERE WEREN'T NO YELLOW CAKE URANIUM OR NOTHIN' LIKE THAT...

"THIS THING HERE IS AN ACTUAL GENIE. I WORKED FOR AN OUTFIT IN THE ARMY FIGHTING THINGS MOST PEOPLE THINK AIN'T REAL."
T. CYPRESS
T.P.T.B.
WRITER: MATT NIXON ART: TOBY CYPRESS
LETTERS: MATT KROTZER
RETCON LOGO DESIGN: SAL CIPRIANO

IS THAT THING FREAKIN' REAL?
THIS IS GOING UP ON INSTAGRAM. HASHTAG: FREAKY!

MY PARTNER ON THE OP WAS JOSH LAKE. CODE NAME: SKINWALKER. HE CAN REMOTELY PILOT ANY VULNERABLE SUBJECT FROM HUNDREDS OF MILES AWAY.
HE WAS USING PEOPLE'S BODIES AGAINST THEIR WILL. HE DISGUSTED ME. I ONLY TOOK THIS GIG TO WIPE OUT A D.U.I. SO I COULD GET A REAL JOB.

THIS IS ROSS. HE'S SHOWING THEM A GODDAMN PICTURE. CAN VERIFY: CAT'S OUT OF THE BAG. SHOULD WE BRING HIM IN?

I DISGUSTED ME.
SANCTION? WHY? NO--BUT HE'S AN OLD MAN--WE CAN HANDLE HIM.

SWEEP THE ROOM? NO, WE SURE AS HELL WON'T KILL INNOCENT PEOPLE!

BECAUSE OF MY UNIQUE BURDEN, I WAS RECRUITED BY THESE MEN. I JOINED THEIR TEAM, BUT THIS WAS NOT SOMETHING THAT I AGREED TO. I'M NO MURDERER OF OLD VETERANS.

COPY THAT.

WHAT DID YOU SAY YOUR JOB WAS IN THE ARMY?
I WAS WITH THE P.O.D.--KIND OF LIKE A SUPERNATURAL BOMB SQUAD...
WHENEVER SOME TIN POT DICTATOR TRIED TO WEAPONIZE SOMETHING PARANORMAL, LIKE THIS HERE, THEY SENT US.

THEY WANTED ME TO HELP KILL AN OLD MAN FOR BEING LONELY AND LOOKING FOR SUPPORT. FUCK THAT.

SOMETHING WAS ROTTEN IN THE CHAIN OF COMMAND AND I'D SENSED IT SINCE I WAS RECRUITED.

I'M NOT MILITARY MATERIAL. I TOLD THEM THAT, BUT THEY INSISTED THAT MY ABILITIES WERE USEFUL TO THEM. I MEAN, FOUR MONTHS AGO I WAS JUST A FUCKING BARISTA, OKAY?

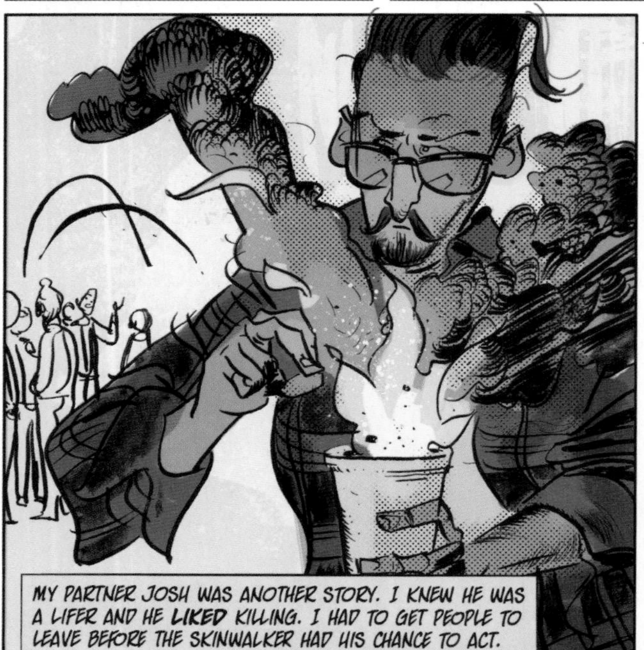
MY PARTNER JOSH WAS ANOTHER STORY. I KNEW HE WAS A LIFER AND HE LIKED KILLING. I HAD TO GET PEOPLE TO LEAVE BEFORE THE SKINWALKER HAD HIS CHANCE TO ACT.

FIRE! FIRE! RUN!

FIRE? OH MY GOD!
OH MY GOD!
FIRE! EVERYONE OUT! THERE'S A FIRE IN THE ROOM--GET THE HELL OUT OF HERE!

FIRE?! WHAT SORT OF FUCKERY IS THIS?

THAT AIN'T NO FIRE! WHAT THE HELL DO YOU THINK YER DOING?
THERE'S A FIRE AND I'M TRYING TO GET PEOPLE OUT OF DANGER!

SON, ARE YOU SOME KIND OF PUSSY?! AIN'T NO DANGER! JUST DROP THAT CUP ON THE GROUND AND STOMP IT OUT!
JUST HOLD ON, SERGEANT DODGE! LET THESE PEOPLE CLEAR OUT.

H-HOW DO YOU KNOW ME? DO YOU WORK FOR THEM? D-DO YOU!?
GOVERNMENT'S STILL KEEPING TABS ON ME, EH? THOUGHT I SMELLED A SPOOK IN THE ROOM!

THE PLACE WAS A FIRETRAP--ONE WAY IN, ONE WAY OUT. DIDN'T KNOW PEOPLE WOULD PANIC LIKE THAT... THE SMOKE WAS JUST SUPPOSED TO BE A DIVERSION.

AND THE BOMB WE WERE SENT TO DEFUSE WAS BLOWING UP IN MY FACE.

ROAR!
HOLY FUCKING SHIT!

GRRRAH!

AND **THAT'S** WHEN JOSH MADE HIS MOVE AND HE CLEARLY WASN'T WITH ME ON MY DECISION TO BE INSUBORDINATE.
COME ON, BRANDON. QUIT SCREWING AROUND AND GET REAL. THIS SANCTION IS GOING TO HAPPEN!

THIS HAS BEEN VERY NTERTAINING, SEEING YOU CHANGE INTO A WEREBEAR AND ALL, BUT SERGEANT CHRIS DODGE, YOU HAVE BEEN ***DISAVOWED.***
RAWR!
JOSH, **STOP!** WHAT ARE YOU DOING? WE CAN'T DO THIS!

FOR SURE WE CAN DO THIS--IT'S A BIT ***SLOW,*** SURE. BUT THIS SILVER-ASED NANITE TECH WORKS LIKE A **CHARM** AGAINST LYCANTHROPES.
WHICH HE TOTALLY IS. THESE WILL EAT HIM ALIVE.

SERGEANT DODGE!

STH-UT UPF
CLONK
I'M WITH THE SAME UNIT TH--

RRRR-OAR!

HORRIBLE SILVER NANO-SWARM, *I CHOOSE YOU!*

SPAK

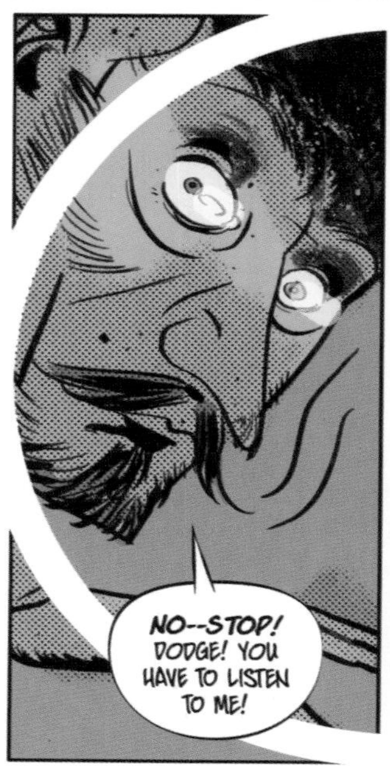
NO--STOP! DODGE! YOU HAVE TO LISTEN TO ME!

WHAT THE FUCK IS THAT THING?
WHO FUCKING CARES?! MOVE, FATASS!

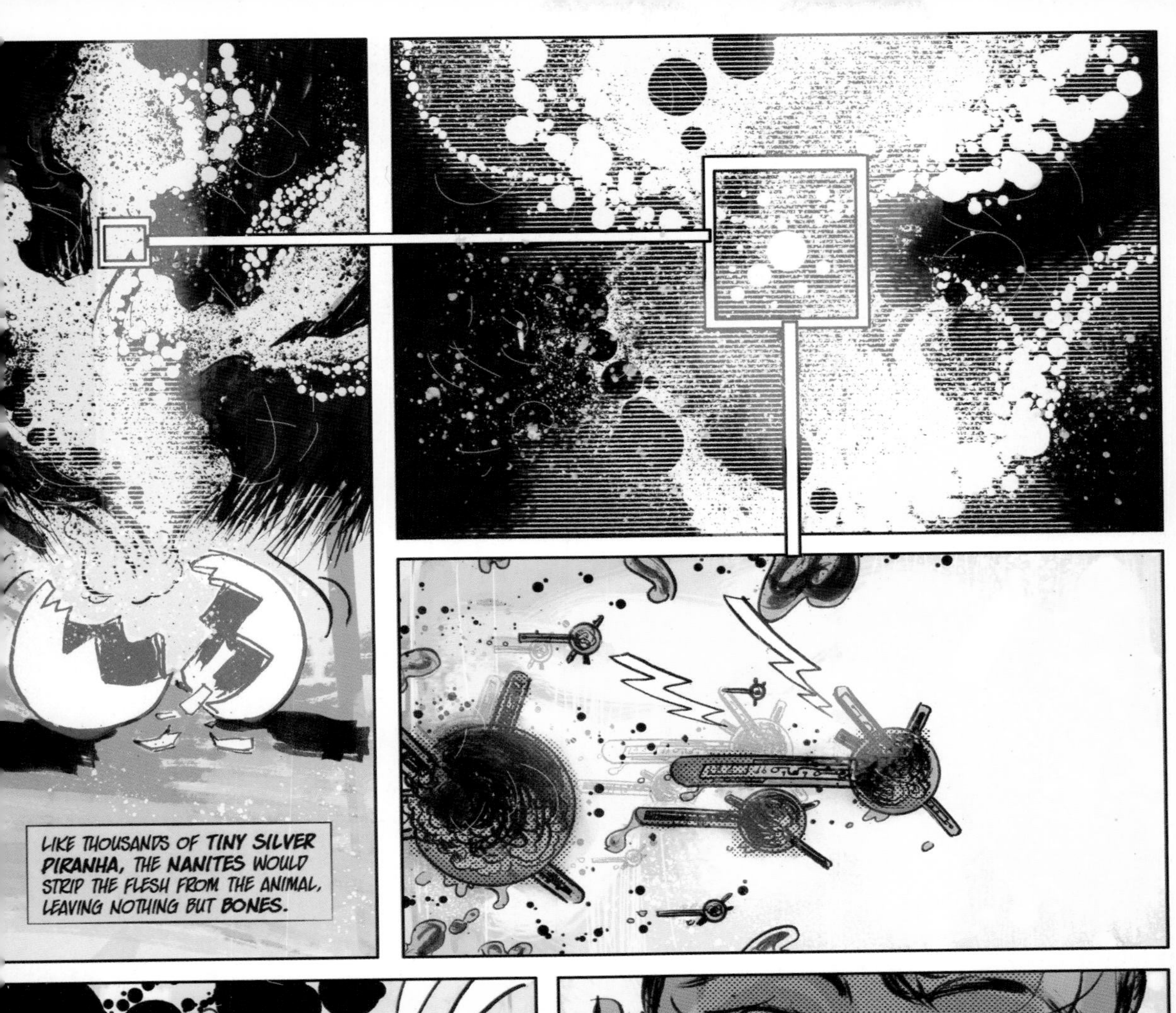
LIKE THOUSANDS OF TINY SILVER PIRANHA, THE NANITES WOULD STRIP THE FLESH FROM THE ANIMAL, LEAVING NOTHING BUT BONES.

I SHOULD HAVE STAYED DOWN. BY FOCUSING THE ATTACK WITH HIS REMOTE TRANSMITTER, THE SKINWALKER WAS ABLE GET THE ANIMAL'S ATTENTION OFF OF HIM AND BACK ON ME.
DODGE, YOU HAVE TO FOCUS. RETURN TO YOUR ORIGINAL FORM--THAT'S THE ONLY WAY TO GET THEM OFF OF YOU!
NO! I'M TRYING TO HELP YOU. YOU HAVE TO CALM DOWN.

DODGE--WAIT! THAT WOMAN OVER THERE--MY PARTNER; SHE'S UNDER ORDERS TO KILL YOU!

GIVE IT UP, BRAND. YOU KNOW ALL I HAVE TO DO IS APPLY A LITTLE MORE PRESSURE AND...

ROAR!!

SHIT. UNNNG. NO! DON'T MAKE ME DO THIS, DODGE!
THUMP

YOU'RE JUST LIKE A LITTLE BABY BIRD WHO'S BEEN THROWN INTO THE CANYON TOO SOON, AREN'T YOU, BRAND?
YOU JUST AREN'T READY TO FLY YET.
BUT I KNOW YOU CAN HIT. LET'S SEE IT.

PLEASE!

WELL THAT'S ENOUGH OF **THAT.**
SEE, I HAVE THIS... **UNUSUAL** THING ABOUT ME.

WHEN I'M IN TROUBLE, I HAVE THIS ONBOARD PERSONALITY WHO SORT OF TAKES OVER.

NOT COMPLETELY. I'M STILL THERE BUT IT'S LIKE I'M WATCHING IT HAPPEN. IT ISN'T ANGER OR RAGE.

IT'S SOMETHING COLD AND EFFICIENT. ANCIENT AND UNFORGIVING. IT DOES WHAT IT HAS TO DO TO PROTECT US. IT DOES WHAT IT MUST TO ENSURE THAT ITS VEHICLE SURVIVES AND THEN IT RELENTS.

IT ISN'T JUST MONSTER ARMS OR STEEL-HARD SKIN, IT CAN MAKE ME INTO ANYTHING THAT WILL SUIT ITS PURPOSE.

SHE CALLS HERSELF "MERRY SUE."

AND TOGETHER WITH THE NANITES, WE REALLY DID A NUMBER ON CHRIS "THE ANIMAL" DODGE. SO MUCH FOR HONORING AMERICA'S HEROES. THIS WAS A NIGHTMARE.
AAGGHHAAAAGGAAAAAGGH

YOU ABOUT READY TO GO, BRAND?

HE WAS GOING TO BLOW IT ALL UP, ME WITH IT. HE KNEW THAT MERRY SUE WOULD PROTECT ME FROM THE BLAST.

NOT A BAD PLAN, DESTROY ALL THE EVIDENCE AND COVER OUR TRACKS IN ONE SHOT.
BUT I COULDN'T LET IT HAPPEN.

REALLY? YOU'RE GOING TO SHOOT ME? YOU KNOW I'M GOING TO BURN THIS BODY ANYHOW. YOU WANT TO KILL ME? GO AHEAD!
EVEN IF I WERE THE TYPE, I WASN'T SURE THAT KILLING HIM WAS ACTUALLY POSSIBLE.
FOR ALL I KNEW HE'D JUST WAKE UP BACK IN HIS OWN BODY IN A FEW HOURS WITH A REALLY BAD HEADACHE. AND THIS GIRL DIES.

THIS IS HOW WE MAKE IT LOOK LIKE AN ACCIDENT AND DELETE ALL EVIDENCE.
EVEN MY BODY.
WELL, SECOND THOUGHT, WE'LL CALL IT A TERRORIST ATTACK. THE OL' **FALSE FLAG.**

THE MEDIA'LL PROBABLY BE TOLD TO GO WITH THAT. NATION COULD **USE** A SHOT OF FEAR.

HE WAS HOLDING A DETONATOR. KNOWING HIM, THE BOMB HE RIGGED COULD KILL EVERYONE ON THE BLOCK.

STOP, JOSH! PLEASE DROP THE DETONATOR! THINK ABOUT WHAT THEY'RE ASKING US TO DO TO THESE PEOPLE!
GAH!

WAIT!
SPAK

B-BZZ
BAZZ

MOM? MOM, WHERE **AM** I? WHERE IS THIS--
ZZT

HELP... PLEASE.
OH MY GOD.

WHAT HAPPENED NEXT IS EXACTLY WHY WE HAVE TO GET ME OUT OF THIS POPULATED SPACE RIGHT NOW. I THOUGHT THIS WAS IT--BUT THESE PEOPLE ARE **RUTHLESS**.

THE PENTAGON.
...YOU'RE A TOTAL COCKSUCKER, BRANDON ROSS.

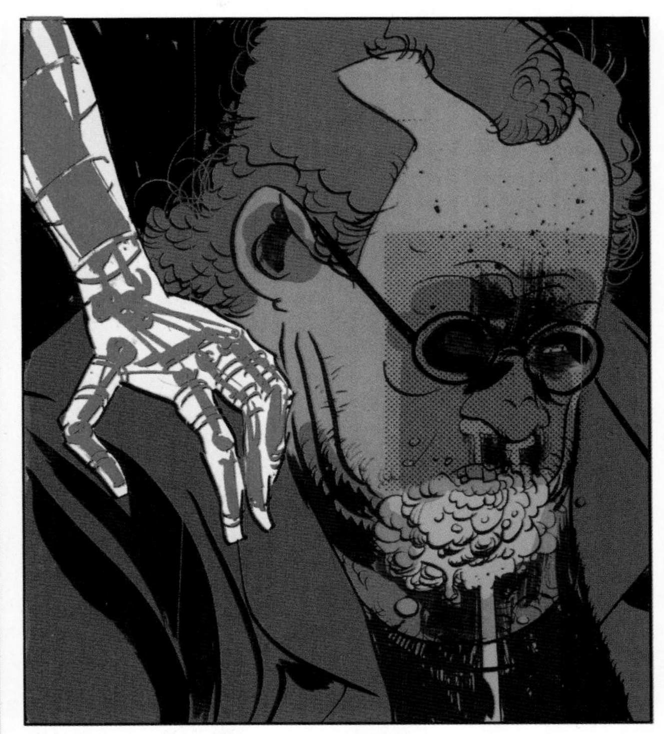

WHAT THE **FUCK**, ABLE?
I'M NOT CERTAIN, SIR. IT APPEARS SOMEBODY BROKE THE LINK TO SKINWALKER'S HOST BODY. AND BOTH MIC REMOTES ARE NOW DOWN.
THUMP
I THINK, BASED ON HIS LAST MANIC REPORT, IT WAS QUITE LIKELY LT. ROSS WHO DID THIS.

GIVE ME A MINUTE. AND GET HIM OUT OF HERE.
YES SIR, COLONEL SWAN.
UR-UNF
I'LL GET A CREW UP HERE RIGHT AWAY.

HUNF. HA! WHO ARE YOU, BOY?

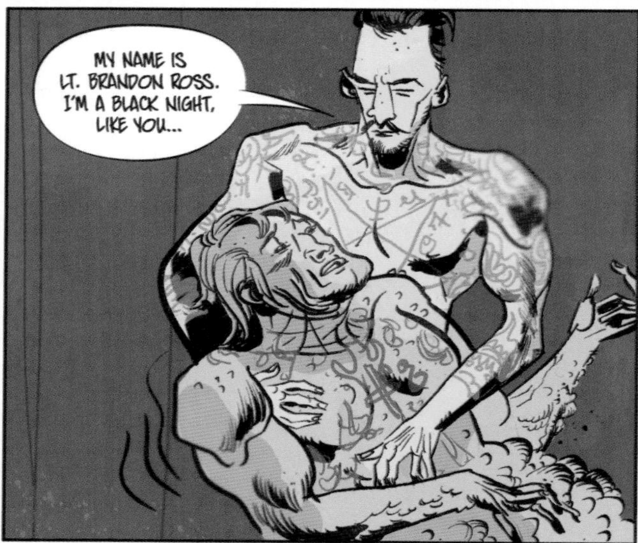
MY NAME IS LT. BRANDON ROSS. I'M A BLACK NIGHT, LIKE YOU...

NO, WHO ARE YOU?

I RECOGNIZED THEM MAGIC WORDS ON YOU. YOU HAVE TO PROTECT HER THAT GAVE 'EM TO YOU. SAME AS SHE PROTECTED US...

WHO? YOU KNOW WHO GAVE ME THE TATTOOS?

OF COURSE I DO! THE PRETTY FRENCH WOMAN IN THE PITCHER.

HE WAS TALKING ABOUT THE DAMN PHOTO... BUT IT WAS GONE BEFORE I'D LOOKED CLOSELY. I KNOW WHO HE WAS TALKING ABOUT.
SHE WAS A FRIEND OF MINE TOO. YOU BETTER FIND HER, BOY... SHE'S NEXT.

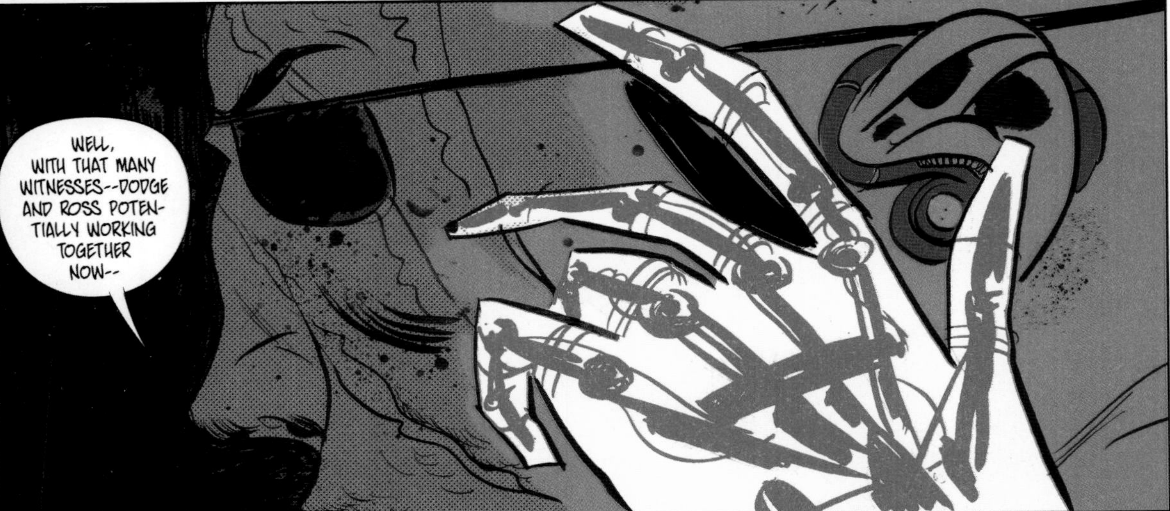
WELL, WITH THAT MANY WITNESSES--DODGE AND ROSS POTENTIALLY WORKING TOGETHER NOW--

I'M CERTAIN THE SILVER NANITES DID THE TRICK WITH CHRIS DODGE.
THE ANIMAL HAS BEEN PUT DOWN. THE PARANORMAL ORDNANCE HAS BEEN EFFECTIVELY DISPOSED OF.
DOESN'T MATTER, WE'RE EXPOSED. I DON'T WANT MY CONSIDERATION FOR THE DRONE PROGRAM REVOKED OVER THIS MESS. DO IT.

THE FAIL-SAFE, SIR?
OVERLOAD THE NANITES. THAT WILL DETONATE THE FAIL-SAFE.

DO IT NOW.

YOUR BOSS--
JESUS!

PUNCH IT, YOU BUREAUCRAT!

BA
BOOM

AND THAT'S WHEN YOUR MEN FOUND ME STANDING THERE IN A BLAST CRATER.
I THINK I DID SOME STUFF THE WRONG WAY BUT I STILL THINK I DID THE RIGHT THING.
N.Y.P.D.
YOU WANT TO KNOW WHAT I THINK?

YES.

YOU'RE A BOMBER, I SAYS, A TERRORIST WHO CAME BACK TO SEE HIS HANDIWORK AND WE CAUGHT YOU.

AIN'T THAT RIGHT, "BRANDON"? OR WHATEVER THE FUCK YOUR NAME REALLY IS...

I CAN SEE WHY YOU THINK THAT, BUT YOU'RE WRONG.

WASHINGTON, D.C.

GOOD EVENING, SIR.

LT. ROSS IS STILL ALIVE. HE'S IN CUSTODY AT A MANHATTAN PRECINCT.

ABLE, YOU ASSHOLE.
WHY THE ***FUCK*** DID IT TAKE SO LONG TO FIND OUT? WHO DO WE HAVE IN NEW YORK?

HARRGG ROOG

SUPER-THERMITE AND A SILVER TIP TEAM ARE ON STANDBY.
HE'LL DO. SEND HIM IN. AND ***ABLE,*** IF YOU CONFERENCE 'PORT INTO MY HOUSE AGAIN, I ***WILL*** SHOOT YOU THE NEXT TIME I SEE YOU IN REAL LIFE.

DETECTIVE CASE? YOU SHOULD LEAVE. YOU SHOULD LEAVE ME HERE AND EVACUATE THIS ENTIRE PRECINCT.

LEAVE?

YOU GOT HIT ON THE HEAD PRETTY HARD.

LOOK, MAN, I'M A TRAITOR. AN ENEMY OF THE STATE. AND RIGHT NOW THEY'RE COMING TO KILL ME.
YOU SHOULD HURRY. YOU'RE RUNNING OUT OF TIME.

CHAPTER TWO

WASHINGTON, D.C.
HRNNG
NNGGH

NNGGHHH
NNNG
COCK-SUCKER!

MOTHER-FUCKER!
HHRRNNGG
CRRNGGHH

HHRRNNGG
CRRNGGHH

POP

RATTLE
RATTLE

MUNCH
MUNCH MUNCH

CRRAKT

CLIC
SHADOW-RUN

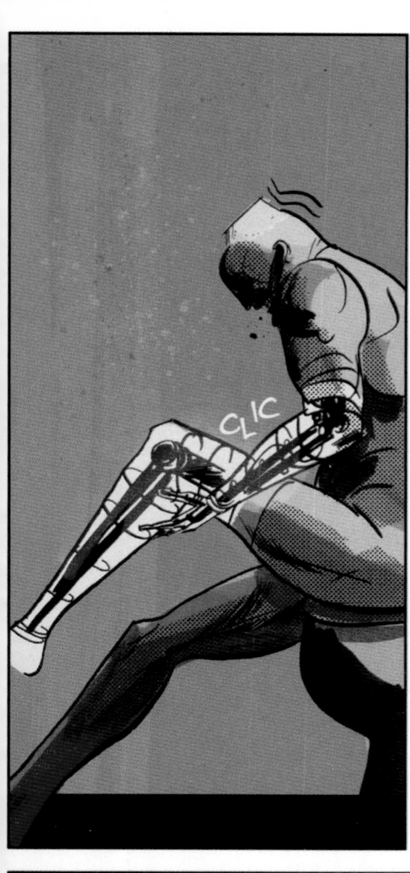
CLIC

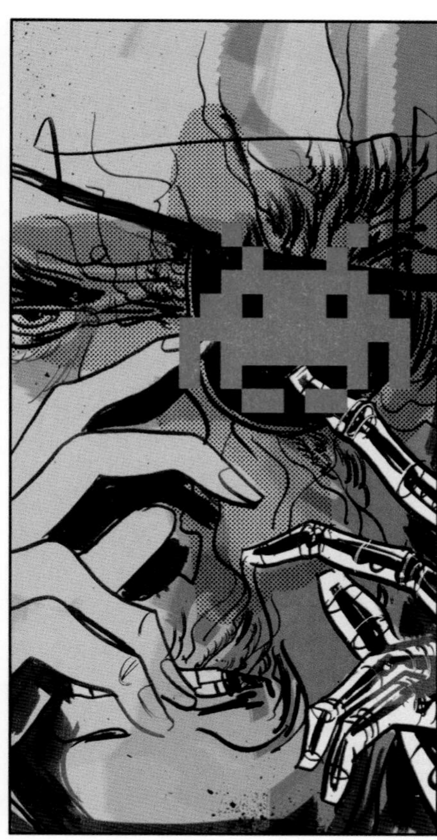

TIME TO GO TO WORK.

NOK
NOK

KEITH?

HONEY, ARE YOU OKAY?

TALK TO ME...

LYN, I'M POSITIVELY READY TO TAKE ON THE WORLD.

NEW YORK CITY.
LISTEN, MR. CASE--

"DETECTIVE" OR "OFFICER CASE" TO YOU, MR. FUCKING TERRORIST SCUMBAG.

DETECTIVE CASE, ONCE AGAIN I'M TELLING YOU THAT THIS WHOLE BUILDING IS A TARGET.

I DON'T DO A LOT OF SPECULATING. MY ONBOARD DEMON, MERRY SUE, IS PRESCIENT. SHE DOES THE SPECULATING AND SHE'S ALSO WHY I CAN DO THIS...
THE FUCK ARE YOU DOING?

SHE JUST HELPED ME TRANSMUTE THE OFFICE CRAP ON YOUR DESK INTO THESE.
VOILA!

POW!

I DON'T LIKE YOU OR YOUR DAMN TRICKS, MAGIC MOTHERFUCKER! DAVID BLAINE'S BEEN MAKING SHIT OUT OF STUFF FOR YEARS. IT'S ALL TRICKS!

MEANWHILE IN D.C.
STARBUCKS COFFEE
LISTEN, ABLE-- JUST GET IT TOGETHER. HE CAN'T HAVE GOTTEN FAR...

DEEP ROAST!
LATTE...
PLEASE... NO talking on cell Phones -managment
WELL, I SEE, IF THE POLICE HAVE HIM, THEN WE HAVE HIM...

COFFEE-- BLACK.

HITTING ME WON'T ACCOMPLISH ANYTHING. I'VE TOLD YOU EVERYTHING. AND I'M TIRED OF BEING HIT TODAY.

DON'T LISTEN TO ME, FINE.
BUT MY DEMON TELLS ME THEY ARE GOING TO TRY ANOTHER BRUTE FORCE ATTACK. BUT JUST MORE POWERFUL. BECAUSE, THEY THINK THAT WILL WORK.

WHY IS IT ALWAYS "THEY" AND "THEM" WITH YOU GUYS? G.I. GODDAMN JOE, THE MUFFIN MAN, FREAKING NINJA SANTA CLAUS AND HIS MERRY FREAKING ELVES--I DON'T GIVE A SHIT WHO THEY ARE, MOTHERFUCKER...

THE ATTACK WILL KILL EVERYONE ON THE BLOCK. **EXCEPT ME.**

WE'LL SEE ABOUT THAT.

WE ALL LOST BROTHERS ON NINE-ELEVEN AND NOW WE WANT US A LITTLE TERRORIST PAYBACK.
BOYS, CAREFUL. THIS CLOWN SAYS HE'S POSSESSED BY DEMONS.

NO, I POSSESS IT. I'M ITS CAGE.
OKAY, DEMON BOY--WE'RE GOING FOR A RIDE.

YES, YES THAT'S IT!

NYPD
PERFECT, YES, LET'S GO FOR A RIDE! GET ME AS FAR AWAY FROM INNOCENT PEOPLE AS POSSIBLE. MAY I HAVE MY GLASSES, PLEASE?

RIIPTT
MAN, THIS GUY'S A IDIOT! DON'T KNOW WHAT'S GOOD FOR HIM.

ABLE, I SWEAR TO CHRIST! HE'S IN THAT PRECINCT BUILDING, OTHERWISE CAMERAS WOULD HAVE CAUGHT HIM. SOME HOTDOGS FROM THE STATION TOOK HIM OFF GRID, PROTECTING THEIR "COLLAR", MARK MY WORDS.

GENERAL NARCISSUS
USE A BIGGER BOMB, YOU DICKHEAD! SEND SUPER-THERMITE LIKE I ORDERED. THIS IS A TOTAL WIPE.

STEP ASIDE, PEOPLE.

WE GOT A DISEASE BAG HERE.

THE HECK IS *THIS* BULL CRAP?

NOW JUST A MINUTE, DARN IT!

CASE! CASE, DON'T YOU IGNORE ME, DETECTIVE! JUST WHAT THE HECK IS GOING ON HERE?

WE GOT OURSELVES A FUCKING EBOLA MONKEY, CHIEF! GOT TO GET HIM TO THE HOSP--

LANGUAGE, DETECTIVE-- I'VE WARNED YOU ABOUT THE FOUL MOUTH!
WELL, THIS SURE AS SHOOT ISN'T THE WAY THINGS ARE DONE IN THIS PRECINCT!

ISOLATE HIM FIRST AND CALL THE C.D.C., THEN CALL E.M.S., AND ALERT THE HOSPITAL NEXT!

LOOK, HEY, CHIEF, IN A FEW MINUTES THE F.B.I. WILL BE HERE TO TAKE THAT BOMBER WE HAVE DOWN IN LOCK-UP... WE CAN'T HAVE THEM EXPOSED TO THIS JACKASS, CAN WE?

YES, OF COURSE YOU'RE RIGHT. GET THAT GUY OUT OF HERE. WE HAVE A BIG CATCH TO SERVE UP, DON'T WE?

WHAT DID YOU SAY THAT INFECTED GUY IN THE HELMET JUST DID? WHAT CRIME?

WHO? EBOLA MAN? HE TRIED TO RAPE A NUN.

GOOD GOD! WHILE INFECTED WITH EBOLA?!
YES, SIR! SAID HE HATES JESUS, LOVES BATH SALTS AND EVERYTHING. SICK FUCKER RIGHT THERE...

JUST GET BACK HERE ON THE ASAP.

SHIT.

NY1

AUTO
PILOT
ENGAG
DISENG

SLAM

LOCK AND BURN ALL PHONES AND AUDIO/VIDEO SURVEILLANCE IN THE AO. EMP BURN, SIX-BLOCK RADIUS. I'M SHIELDED.

HEY!

I'M CLEAR...

PRECINCT
POLICE

KLAK
KLAK

BA-BOOM

SEEDING BOGUS SYRIAN PASSPORTS. HAHA, FUCKING MIGRANTS...

SYRIENNE

CLOTHE

IF YOU'RE READY TO HEAR ME OUT, DETECTIVE CASE... I HAVE A PLAN.

WE NEED TO FIND THE WOMAN IN THE PICTURE THAT THE ANIMAL BROUGHT TO THE AA MEETING.

ELSEWHERE.

MANHATTAN IS **AGAIN** IN FLAMES.

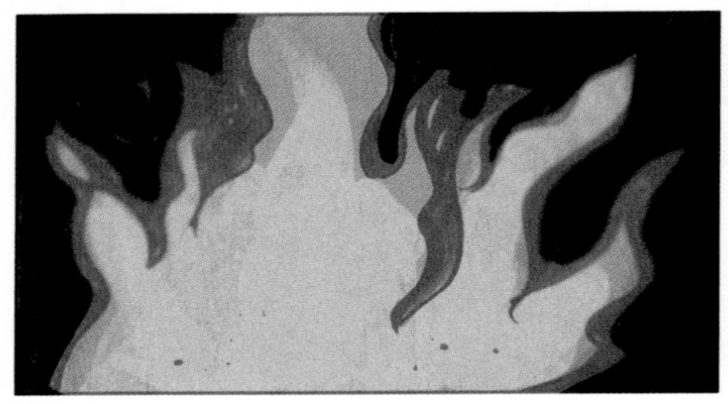

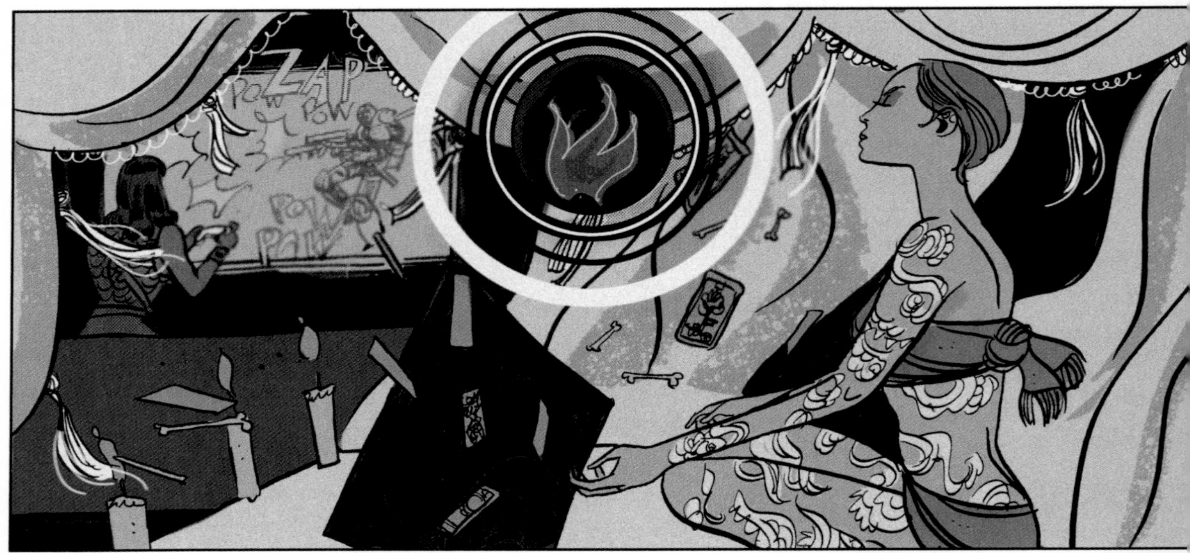
ZAP
POW

POW
POW
KRUSH
POWER MOVE
WE GOING TO BUST SOME HEADS? I **LOVE** NEW YORK!

NO, WE ARE GOING TO **DINE.** WHEN THE TIME COMES, WE WILL FIND EACH OTHER.

THE WOMAN, SHE GAVE US OUR TATTOOS--TO PROTECT US.
ME AND CHRIS "THE ANIMAL" DODGE GOT THEM FROM HER. SHE'S THE WORLD'S GREATEST WITCH. AN IMMORTAL.
NYPD

SHE WAS ON THIS PARANORMAL ORDNANCE DISPOSAL TEAM FOR **DECADES,** STARTING WITH WORLD WAR II. SHE FOUGHT THE FUCKING **NAZIS,** MAN!
YOU'RE SAYING THE GUYS ON THE **PARA-WHAT-HAVE-YOU** SQUAD ARE LED BY A **WITCH** AND YOU'RE A **DEMON HANDLER?** WHY ARE THEY TRYING TO BLOW YOU UP LIKE THIS? IT'S **SLOPPY.** WE LOST **GOOD MEN** IN THERE! **AGAIN!**

THEY'RE PANICKING BECAUSE I PICKED UP ON SOMETHING. SOMETHING IS **OFF** WITH OUR COMMANDING OFFICER. HAS BEEN FOR MONTHS. HIS BEEF WITH THE ANIMAL WAS **PERSONAL.**
AND THE PERSON WHO KNEW HIM **BEST** IS MADAME ALEXANDRA DAVID-NEEL.

OKAY, WE'RE LISTENING.

WASHINGTON, D.C.

THIS GODDAMN COMMUTE IS KILLING ME, SON!
SIR, YES SIR!

TZZZ

SIR?

I'M FINE. MUST JUST BE A GLITCH.
MAYBE IT HAS SOMETHING TO DO WITH THE ATTACKS IN NEW YORK? HEARD ABOUT SOME EMPS!

NO, SON I THINK THEY'LL FIND OUT THESE WERE A COUPLE OF THOSE ISIS BOYS WHO GOT AHOLD OF TOO MUCH COWSHIT. THEY AIN'T USING THAT KIND OF TECH.
SIR! YES, SIR!

GENERAL SWAN! GENERAL?

I DIDN'T TELL YOU TO **NUKE** A POLICE STATION, YOU ASSHOLE.

SIR? YES, SIR, YOU **DID**.
FUCK OFF, ABLE.

THE FUCK WAS *THAT?*

THAT WAS ME TALKING TO THE DEFENSE NET DURING THE RETINA SCAN.
I FOUND IT. **AT LAST.** I'VE FOUND MY WAY IN. WE'RE NEARLY THERE.

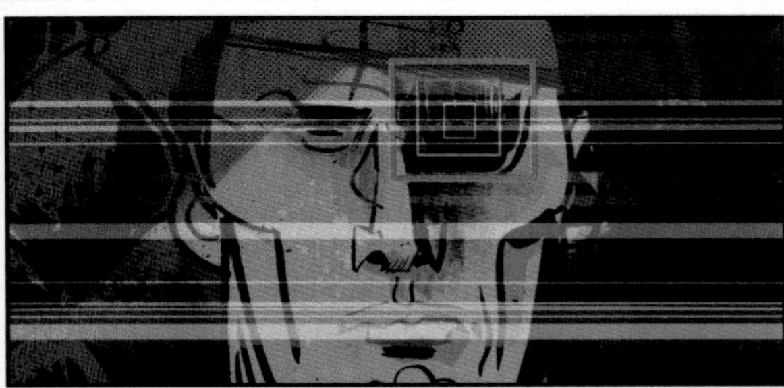

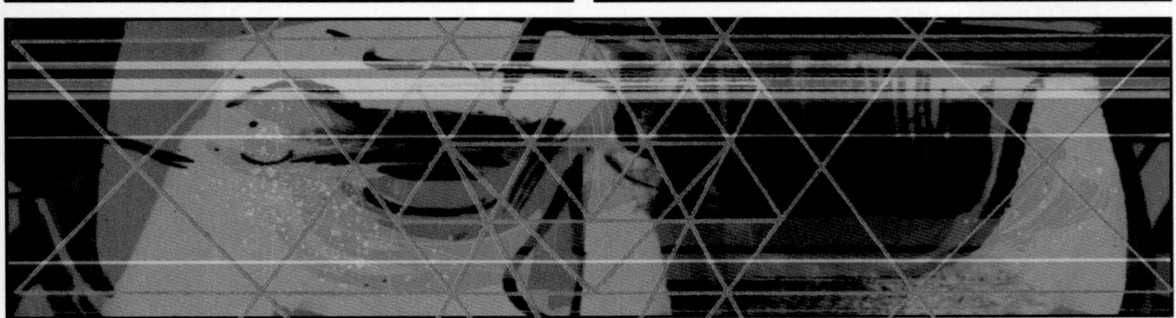

OKAY. GREAT.

FUCK YOU, CASE. I'M GOING TO GREASE THIS MOTHERFUCKER LIKE WE PLANNED AND THEN I'M GOING BACK TO THE STATION TO DIG OUR BOYS OUT. I DON'T GIVE A FUCK WHAT YOU TWO DO.

THUD

NO, YOU'RE NOT!

WHAT THE FUCK?!

HELP!

ALRIGHT, PUSSY, IT'S TIME TO THROW DOWN.

I'D RATHER NOT.

WHAT THE FUCK?!
YOU CAN FLY?
APPARENTLY... YES.
GET BACK HERE, YOU SISSIES! FIGHT ME!

CHAPTER THREE

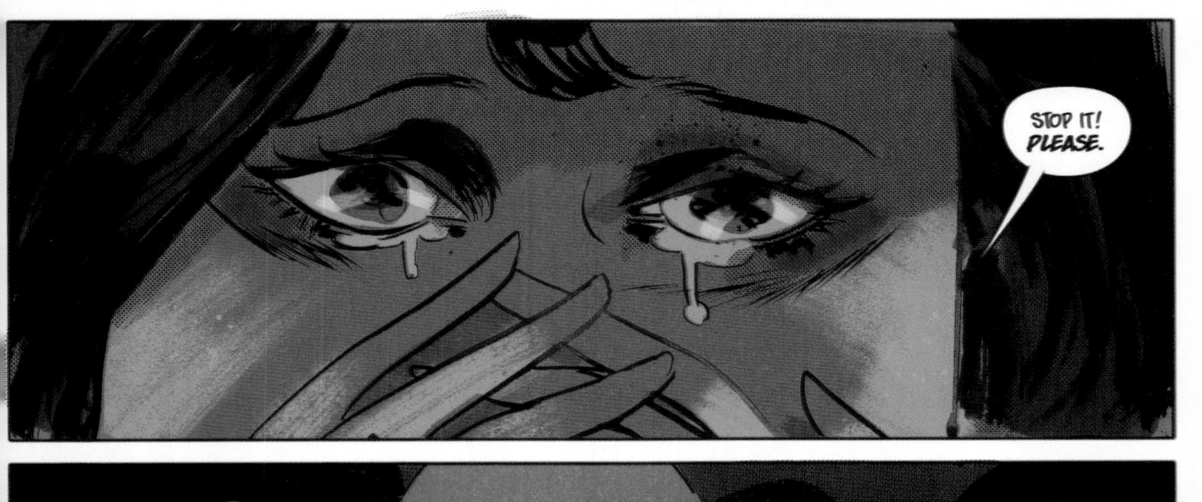
STOP IT! PLEASE.

CHRIS? WOULD YOU PLEASE TAKE MRS. ROSS OUT INTO HER LIVING ROOM AND ASK HER SOME QUESTIONS ABOUT THE EARLY AND SUDDEN DEATH OF MR. ROSS?
AND, PLEASE BE A DEAR AND PUT A KETTLE ON BOIL.

C'MON, MA'AM--YOUR BOY WILL BE **FINE.** THIS IS WHAT WE DO. WE'RE LIKE A BOMB SQUAD FOR THINGS THAT ARE PARANORMAL IN NATURE, SO REALLY, YOU HAVE THE BEST PERSONNEL HANDLING THIS SITUATION.

NOW, MR. CROWLEY-- I'M PROMISING THIS WOMAN THAT HER BABY IS GOING TO BE OKAY, AND I DO **NOT** BREAK PROMISES.
YES, I'M SURE.
ALEISTER, I TOLD YOU THAT MAN HAS A **BEAR** OF A TEMPER, AND SINCE I'VE **JUST** PULLED YOU IN FROM THE PAST, YOU ARE **NOT** VERY STRONG, MAGICALLY SPEAKING.

I AM NOT AFRAID OF SOME **RUN-OF-THE-MILL** SHAPESHIFTER, MY DEAR.

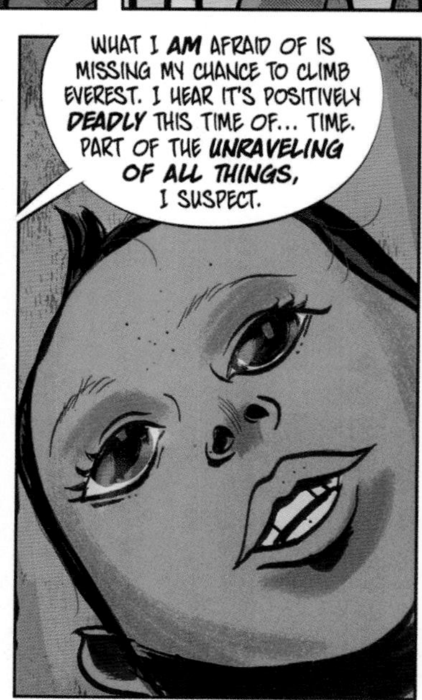
WHAT I **AM** AFRAID OF IS MISSING MY CHANCE TO CLIMB EVEREST. I HEAR IT'S POSITIVELY **DEADLY** THIS TIME OF... TIME. PART OF THE **UNRAVELING OF ALL THINGS,** I SUSPECT.

QUITE. NOW IF YOU HELP ME DO THIS, I'LL FLY YOU TO BASECAMP MYSELF. BUT AFTER THAT, BACK IN TIME YOU GO. FRANKLY, I FIND YOUR CALMNESS UNNERVING.

"I'M SURE YOU DO, MADAME DAVID-NEEL. BUT THIS SORT OF THING IS WHAT MAKES ALEISTER CROWLEY, WELL... **ME.**"
NOW, MA'AM, CAN YOU TELL ME ABOUT THE NIGHT YOUR HUSBAND DIED?
YES, OUR BABY BOY... HE KILLED RICK.

THE BABY WAS JUST PLAY SLAPPING AT HIS DADDY BECAUSE RICK WANTED HIM TO STOP HIS TANTRUM BY **HUGGING IT OUT!** NOT WITH **THAT** BABY, NO, I'M SORRY, I **LOVE** HIM, BUT HE'S A **MONSTER.**
HIS HANDS TURNED INTO TINY FREAKING **SWORDS!** LITTLE BLACK, BONY-LOOKING SWORDS! HE LOOKED LIKE EDWARD SCISSORHANDS!
R'YOU SERIOUS? **HO**-LEEE.
HE JUST CUT RICK TO RIBBONS. **I** WAS BLAMED, OF COURSE. NO ONE BELIEVED ME AND IT BROKE ME TO PAY THE LAWYERS WHO GOT ME A MISTRIAL. GOT ME MY BOY BACK.

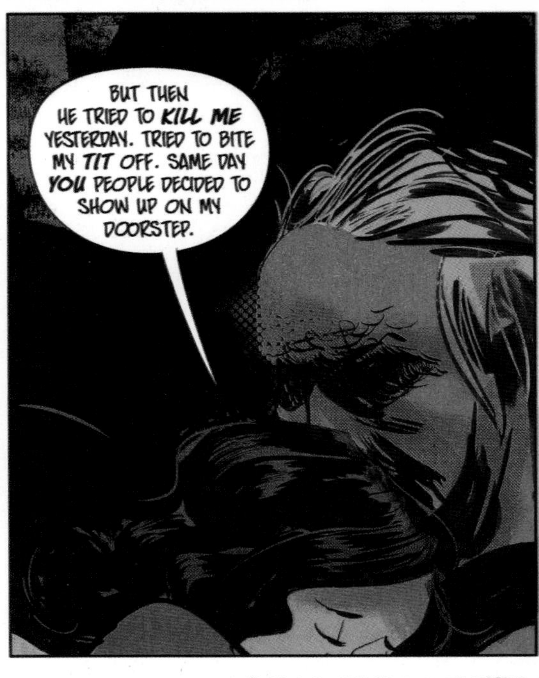
BUT THEN HE TRIED TO **KILL ME** YESTERDAY. TRIED TO BITE MY **TIT** OFF. SAME DAY **YOU** PEOPLE DECIDED TO SHOW UP ON MY DOORSTEP.

WHAT'S THIS INK YOU BROUGHT?
IT'S THE **BLOOD OF CHRIST** MIXED WITH A POUNDED LOCK OF HAIR THAT COMES FROM THE VERY **DEMON** THAT ABIDES IN THIS BOY.

FUCK YOU, THE BLOOD OF CHRIST, MY BALLS! WHY NOT JUST SACRIFICE HIM TO OUR RESPECTIVE GODS AND LET IT BE?
THAT SHOULD TELL YOU THE LEVEL OF THREAT WE ARE DEALING WITH, ALEISTER. THIS BABY IS GOING TO GROW UP TO BE THE BOMB THAT I NEED.
BY MAKING THE DEMON **MERRY SUE** JUST AS POSSESSED OF HIM AS HE IS HER, WE'LL DESTROY OUR ENEMY BEFORE IT OVERWHELMS THE SUPERSTRUCTURE OF THIS PLANET, BEFORE IT CAN LAY WASTE TO WHAT WE CALL REALITY.
BZZZ
BZZZ

TRUST ME, WE'VE DONE THIS BEFORE. HE'S **THE KEY.**
SLEEP, BRANDON ROSS. SLEEP NOW.

WELL, LET'S FINISH TATTOOING THIS BABY SO HE CAN SAVE THE WORLD, AND I CAN GO CLIMB A MOUNTAIN WITHOUT HAVING TO HEAR YOU HARP ON CRYPTICALLY ABOUT YOUR REALITY-ALTERING BAD GUYS.
WICKEDEST MAN ALIVE, ALEISTER?
BZZ
BZZZZZZ

EH.
BZZZZZZZ
TO BE SURE.

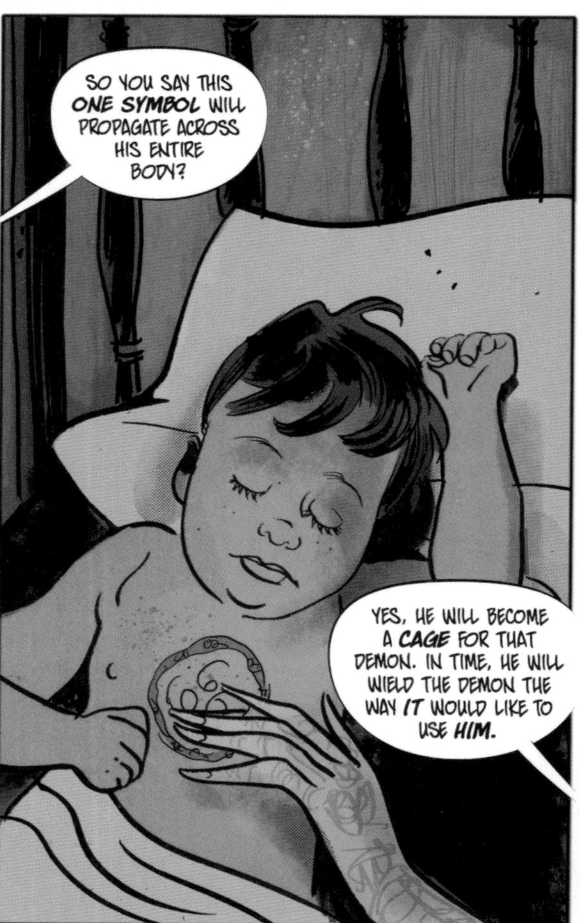
SO YOU SAY THIS **ONE SYMBOL** WILL PROPAGATE ACROSS HIS ENTIRE BODY?
YES, HE WILL BECOME A **CAGE** FOR THAT DEMON. IN TIME, HE WILL WIELD THE DEMON THE WAY *IT* WOULD LIKE TO USE *HIM*.

NOT **CRYING?** THERE'S SOMETHING **QUEER** ABOUT THIS BOY.
HE IS **PERFECT.**

PLEASE GET ME THE FUCK DOWN FROM HERE! C-CAN'T BREATHE... THIN AIR OR SOMETHING. COLD.
THE WEIGHT OF TIME

WE ALMOST GOT HIT B-BY A DAMN JUMBO JET! PLEASE, MAN! I'M GOING TO DIE OF FRIGHT.
I'M DOING THE BEST I CAN... I DON'T THINK I KNOW HOW TO LAND. WE MAY BE IN TROUBLE.

THEY ARE SOMEWHERE DIRECTLY ABOVE JERSEY CITY, DARLING.

THIS ANTIQUATED OLD PIRATE'S TELESCOPE IS NOT WORTH A DAMN, ALEXANDRA. IT NEEDS REPAIR.
MORE TO THE SOUTH, LADY IRONWRATH. YOU MUST SEE THEM.
AND THAT TELESCOPE WAS A GIFT FROM BLACKBEARD HIMSELF. THERE ARE NONE FINER.

WAIT... NO...

I THINK... I SEE HIM. AND THERE SEEMS TO BE A MAN WITH HIM.

WONDERFUL! NOW, LET **ME** SEE.

ZSJAI!

DETECTIVE CASE, I'M NOT SURE WHAT TO DO. EVEN IF I CAN FIGURE HOW TO TAKE US BACK DOWN TO THE CITY, I'LL BE ARRESTED AGAIN, OR THAT PSYCHO WILL COME FOR ME AND **KILL** YOU.
ANYHOW, I'M NOT CLEAR ON MY RANGE--I'VE NEVER FLOWN BEFORE. MAYBE I CAN GET US SOMEWHERE REMOTE.
J-JUST GET ME BACK ON THE GROUND BEFORE I **FREEZE** TO DEATH!

I NEED YOU TO **ANCHOR** ME.

SEEMS A BIT SILLY. I DON'T THINK THIS WILL WORK.
YOU **ALWAYS** SAY THAT ABOUT MAGIC.

WHAT THE FUCK? HANG ON!
HOLY SHIT!
HE MUST BE THREE MILES UP.
AND I'M A SPIRITUAL MAGNET DRAWING HIM IN! HANG ON!

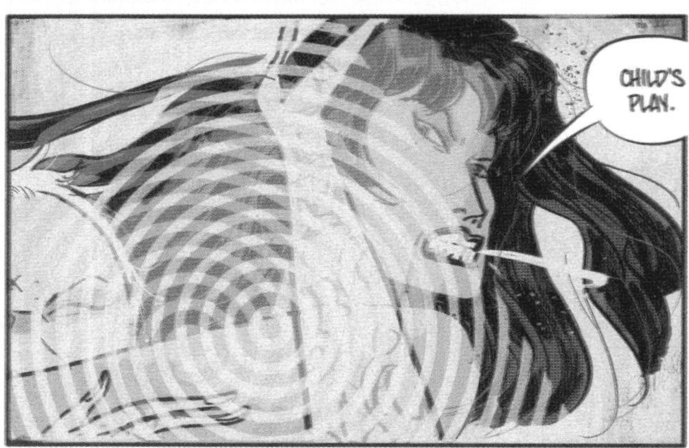
CHILD'S PLAY.

NOW, IRONWRATH!
I GOT IT.

THANK GOODNESS, I'M A LITTLE BURNT.
NOT ME...

UNNGGH

...I AM JUST GETTING HEATED UP.

WELCOME, BRANDON ROSS. IT IS SO NICE TO SEE YOU AGAIN.

AND YOU ARE?

I'M C-CASE. DETECTIVE JOHN CASE.

YOU ARE ABSOLUTELY FROZEN, MY DEAR.

A COP! HOW COOL!

EXCUSE ME...

THE PEOPLE IN MY TRIBE HAVE A **SOLUTION** TO YOUR SHOCK AND CHILL.
THAT OR MAYBE SOME NICE **TEA.**

EXCUSE ME, PEOPLE.
EXCUSE ME! I WANT TO KNOW **WHAT'S** HAPPENING HERE!

YES, DEAR. I'M SORRY--**YOU'RE** THE REAL REASON WE'RE ALL HERE.
PERHAPS WE SHOULD GET INSIDE. I CAN SHIELD THIS SPACE FROM THE PRYING EYES OF **CURRENT** TECHNOLOGY, BUT WHO KNOWS WHAT THEY WILL HAVE BROUGHT WITH THEM THIS TIME.

BACK AT THE PENTAGON.

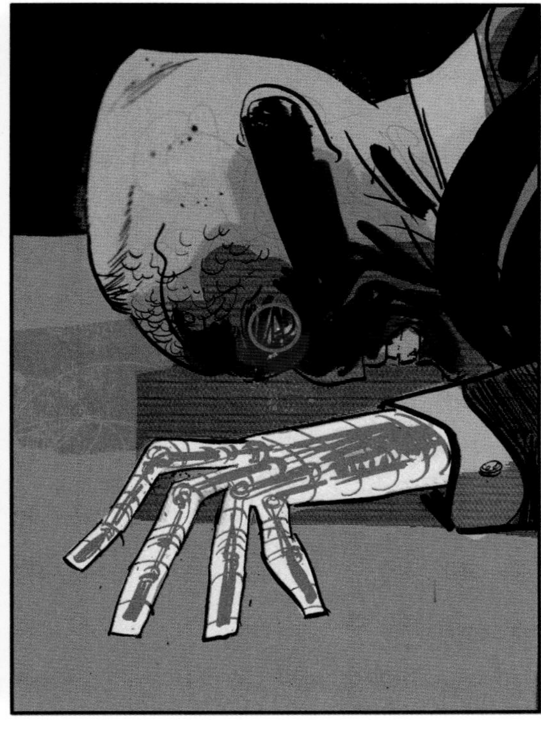

KR·AK

BBZZZZ
BBZZZ

OF COURSE TATTOOING AN INFANT IS VERY FUCKED UP. I AGREE, BRANDON.
HOWEVER, WITHOUT THE TATTOO? THE DEMON YOU CALL "MERRY SUE" WOULD HAVE OVERCOME AND POSSESSED YOU. YOU HAD ALREADY KILLED YOUR OWN FATHER, AND AN EXORCISM WOULD HAVE KILLED YOU OR LEFT YOU BRAIN DEAD.

OR RATHER, IT DID KILL YOU. TWICE. ONCE IT GOT YOU INSTITUTIONALIZED. BRANDON, YOU AND THAT DEMON TOGETHER ARE THE LYNCHPIN IN THIS PARTICULAR GO ROUND.

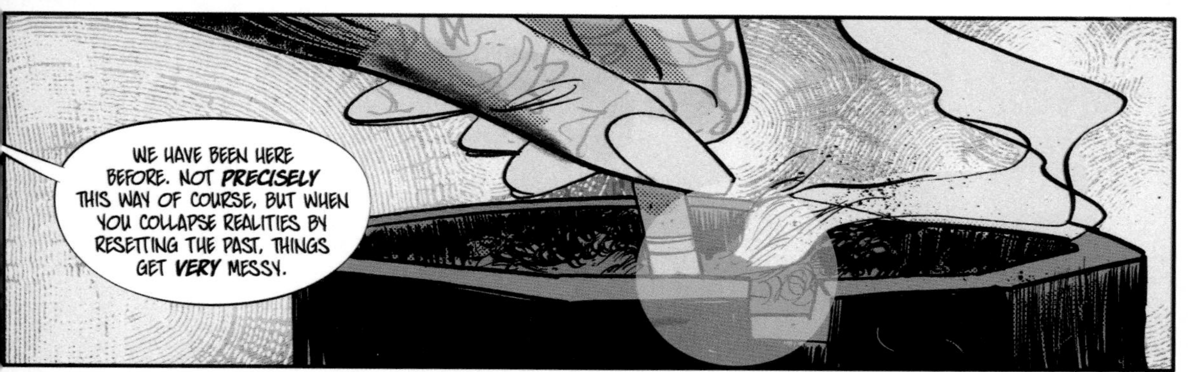
WE HAVE BEEN HERE BEFORE. NOT PRECISELY THIS WAY OF COURSE, BUT WHEN YOU COLLAPSE REALITIES BY RESETTING THE PAST, THINGS GET VERY MESSY.

I'VE MERELY MODIFIED CERTAIN ASPECTS OF YOUR PAST IN ORDER TO PREPARE YOU FOR YOUR BATTLE WITH THE ENTITIES THAT NOW POSSESS KEITH SWAN. IN SOME INSTANCES IT HAD POSSESSED THE MAN SWAN SENT YOU TO KILL. THE ANIMAL.

IT'S A COLONIAL ENTITY THAT IS EXTRATERRESTRIAL IN ORIGIN. WHEN IT TAKES SWAN, IT USES TECHNOLOGY. WHEN IT INHABITS CHRIS "THE ANIMAL" DODGE, IT EXPLOITS NATURE TO STEAL OUR PLANET.

THIS TIME, SWAN IS THE HOST, AND IT WAS TRYING TO USE YOU TO ITS ADVANTAGE. IT HAS ALSO REALIZED THAT OUTRIGHT KILLING YOU IS NOT GOING TO WORK.
HAS IT EVER POSSESSED YOU?

ONCE. THE FIRST TIME IT ARRIVED. AND IT WAS ONLY MOMENTS AFTER THAT THAT OUR TIMELINE RESET ITSELF. I'M LIKE AN AUTOMATIC KILL SWITCH.

SO, TO PREVENT THE END OF OUR WORLD, YOU RESET TIME EVERY TIME WE'VE LOST?
YES.

AND HOW MANY TIMES HAVE YOU DONE THIS?

NINE.

WE'VE NEVER WON?

NO. NOT YET.

COME WITH ME, BRANDON.
THIS TIME WE HAVE A SLIGHT ADVANTAGE IN THAT SWAN ACTUALLY EXPOSED YOU TO SO MANY PARANORMAL EXPERIENCES WITH THE TEAM THAT YOU ARE QUICKER TO ACCEPT THE REALITY IN WHICH YOU FIND YOURSELF. THAT GIVES US MORE TIME FOR YOU TO ACT AGAINST HIM.

WE HAVE A TITANIC HOT TUB DOWN THE HALL. IT IS THIS WAY.
THAT LADY WAS TALKING ABOUT THE WORLD ENDING AND YOU WANT ME TO TAKE A BATH?

YOU ARE A PROTECTOR OF NEW YORK CITY AND YOU DO NOT UNDERSTAND THE VALUE OF RELAXING BEFORE A BATTLE?

BATTLE? I'M GOING TO BE IN A BATTLE?

I HAVE LIVED IN THIS BUILDING FOR A VERY, **VERY** LONG TIME, BRANDON. I BOUGHT THIS FLOOR THE DAY THAT THEY ANNOUNCED IT WOULD BE BUILT. THERE IS **ENERGY** HERE, AND IF YOU ARE THE RIGHT SORT OF PERSON, YOU CAN USE IT TO **GROW** THINGS.

IT CAN ALSO BE USED TO **CONNECT** THINGS, LIKE MEMBERS OF OUR GROUP.

WHAT ARE YOU **KEEPING** IN HERE?

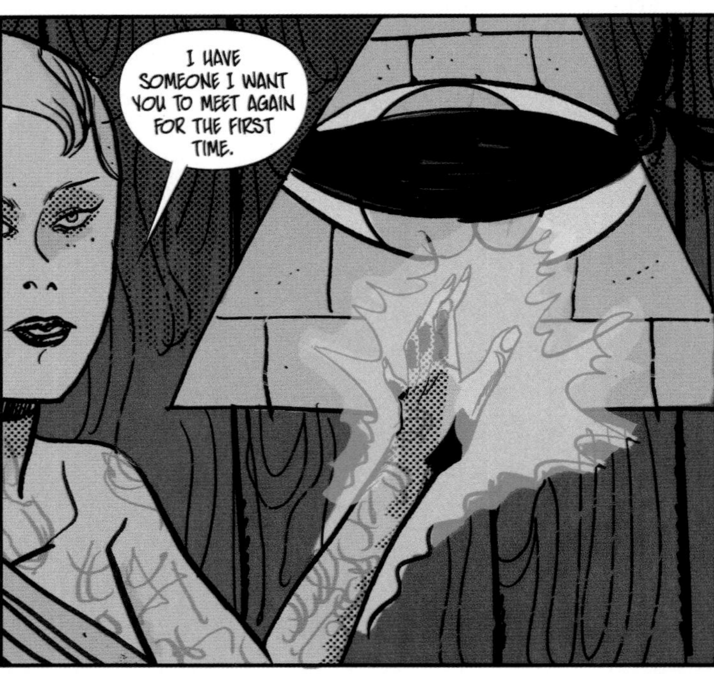
I HAVE SOMEONE I WANT YOU TO MEET AGAIN FOR THE FIRST TIME.

OH MY **GOD**.

HELLO, DEMON BINDER. IT IS GOOD TO SEE YOU AGAIN.

GOOD LUCK, BRANDON.

THEY CALL ME **BIGFOOT**. I AM AN ELEMENTAL BEING, AN ADVOCATE FOR THE **EARTH**. YOUNG MAN, WE HAVE WORK TO DO.

"AT THIS VERY MOMENT, A COLONIAL ENTITY FROM ANOTHER GALAXY IS ATTEMPTING TO INFECT A PENTAGON SUPER COMPUTER. ONCE THAT HAPPENS IT WILL BE CONNECTED TO EVERYTHING...

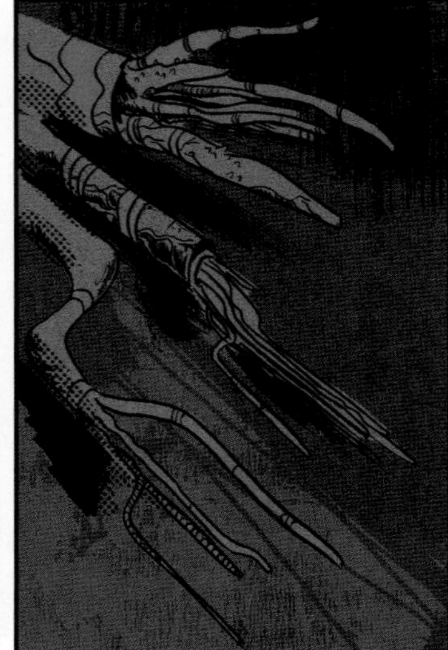

"IN A MATTER OF **MINUTES**, IT WILL HAVE INSTANT ACCESS TO AND POWER OVER DRONES, MISSILES, SATELLITES, FOOD SUPPLY CHAINS."

"AND THAT'S NOT THE **WORST** OF IT. IT WILL HAVE CONTROL OF TECHNOLOGY THAT CAN SPLIT THE EARTH IN TWO."

WHAT A CLICHÉ. WHY **DESTROY** THE PLANET? IT'S A LITTLE **MUSTACHE TWIDDLING** OF THE BAD GUY, ISN'T IT?

AFTER 70,000 SOME YEARS, IT WANTS TO GO HOME.

IT'S GOING TO BLOW UP THE PLANET TO FILL ITS GAS TANK?

SO, TO SPEAK, **YES,** THAT IS HOW THIS PLAYS OUT AND WE NEED **YOU** TO STOP IT.

NOBODY ELSE CAN DO THIS?

NO.

YEAH, OKAY. LET'S DO IT.
I DON'T THINK THERE'S ANY GOING BACK FOR ME. NOT AFTER WHAT I'VE SEEN SWAN DO TO INNOCENT PEOPLE.

HAHA, I DO SEE THAT THERE IS SOMETHING DIFFERENT ABOUT YOU THIS TIME. IT IS THE FIRST TIME THAT YOU HAVE TAKEN SUCH A POSITIVE ATTITUDE.

YEAH, WELL FUCK IT. WHAT KIND OF LIFE DO I HAVE ANYWAY?

YOU HAVE LIFE. THAT IS SOMETHING. AND YOU GIVE IT FREELY. THAT IS EVEN MORE.
TWEET

THANK YOU, DEMON BINDER.
MR. BLUESKY WILL TAKE YOU TO THE ORBITAL RAIL GUN FROM WHICH YOU WILL BE SHOT INTO THE SUPERSTRUCTURE OF THE PENTAGON.

UM, EXCUSE ME, WHAT WAS THAT ABOUT SHOOTING ME FROM A RAILGUN? HELLO, BIGFOOT?

CHAPTER FOUR

JUPITER.
"LOOK, WE DON'T HAVE A LOT OF TIME, SO I'M GOING TO COME OUT AND SAY IT...
"...A SENTIENT SPACECRAFT HAS JUST USED THE LAST OF ITS FUEL TO LEAVE ITS CRASH SITE ON JUPITER."
HERE WE GO AGAIN. AGAIN.

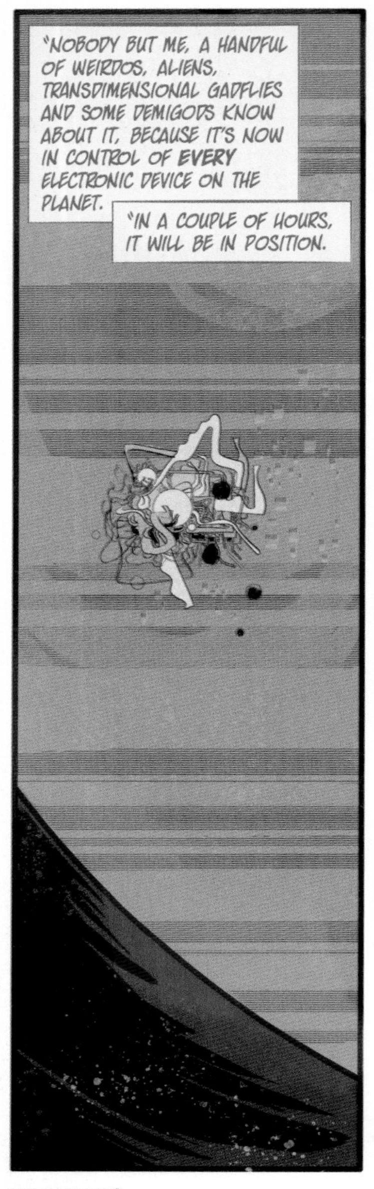
"NOBODY BUT ME, A HANDFUL OF WEIRDOS, ALIENS, TRANSDIMENSIONAL GADFLIES AND SOME DEMIGODS KNOW ABOUT IT, BECAUSE IT'S NOW IN CONTROL OF EVERY ELECTRONIC DEVICE ON THE PLANET.
"IN A COUPLE OF HOURS, IT WILL BE IN POSITION.

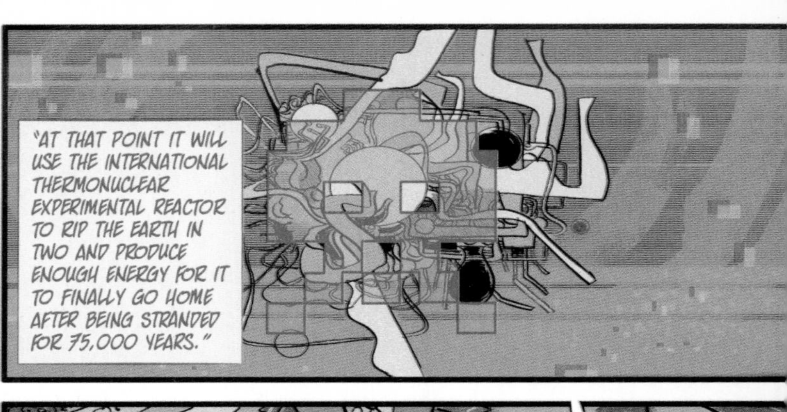
"AT THAT POINT IT WILL USE THE INTERNATIONAL THERMONUCLEAR EXPERIMENTAL REACTOR TO RIP THE EARTH IN TWO AND PRODUCE ENOUGH ENERGY FOR IT TO FINALLY GO HOME AFTER BEING STRANDED FOR 75,000 YEARS."

NEW YORK CITY.
THE DAKOTA.
BASICALLY, IT'S BEEN USING US.

IT JUST WAITED LONG ENOUGH FOR US TO MAKE THIS FUSION REACTOR THING IN FRANCE.

WE'RE ABOUT TO BE BLOWN THE FUCK UP AND YOU STILL THINK THE BEST USE OF OUR TIME IS TAKING A COMMUNAL FUCKING BATH?
I NEED TO MAKE SOME CALLS.

THAT WOULD ACCOMPLISH NOTHING. BY THE TIME YOU CONVINCE ANYONE TO LISTEN TO YOU TELL THEM WHAT I JUST TOLD YOU, IT WILL BE OVER.

THE WORLD ENDS TONIGHT, DETECTIVE CASE...
IT'S OUR JOB TO MAKE SURE THAT WHEN THE DEMON BINDER SHITS THE BED, WE GET A DO-OVER.

AND WE'RE DOING MORE THAN TAKING A BATH!
WHY DOESN'T IT JUST USE THE SUN?

RADIANT SOLAR POWER IS LIMITED, AND THE SHIP IS OUTFITTED FOR A FORM OF COMBUSTION TO TRAVEL. GALACTIC ZONING CODES STATE A SHIP LIKE THAT IS FORBIDDEN TO EVEN APPROACH THE SUN LET ALONE TAMPER WITH IT.
WHAT DO YOU MEAN "GALACTIC ZONING CODES"?

DOWN THE HALL...
PRETTY CRAZY ROOM, EVEN IN THIS BUILDING. FEELS **WEIRD.** IT'S LIKE, I DON'T KNOW--**ALIVE** OR SOMETHING.

I THINK I'M GOING TO BE SICK.

WHAT'S **WRONG**, BOY? **HEY!**

RUMMMBLLE
RRUUNMMNBBI

OH-**KAY** THEN...

ROOOMBLE
RKKAKOOOM
THE HECK?

KKRRMK
ROMMKK
HELLO, BRANDON. SO NICE TO BE IN YOUR LIGHT ONCE AGAIN.

PLEASE, COME WITH US.

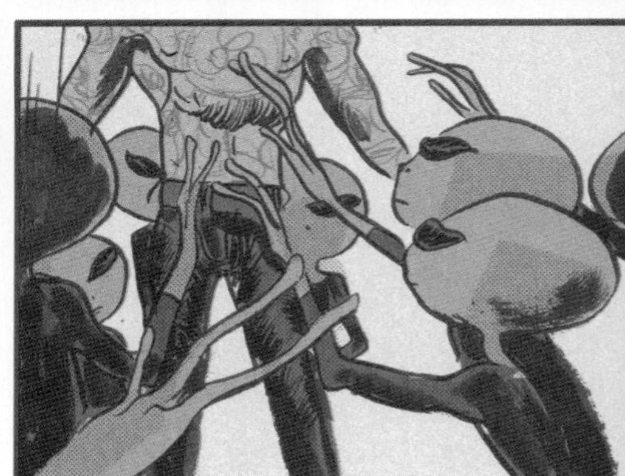

THE PENTAGON.

GENERAL
KEITH SWANN

--THREE! GO! GO! GO!

WHAT THE SHIT IS THIS?

THE FUCK, SARGE? SHOULD WE GREASE THIS SQUATPILE OR WHAT?

ZZORT

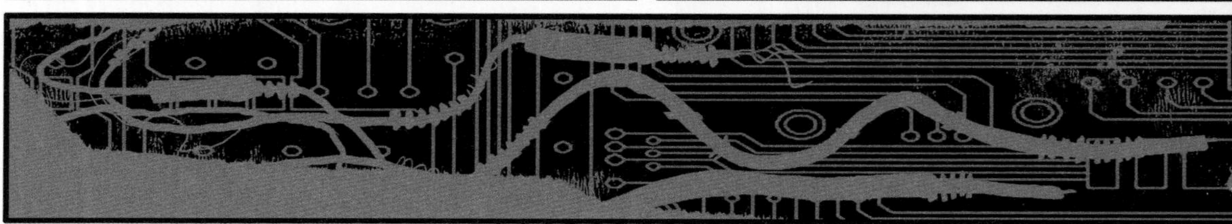

SAINT-PAUL-LÈS-DURANCE, SOUTH OF FRANCE.

INTERNATIONAL THERMONUCLEAR EXPERIMENTAL REACTOR
welcome to ITER:
International Thermonuclear Experimental React

ITER

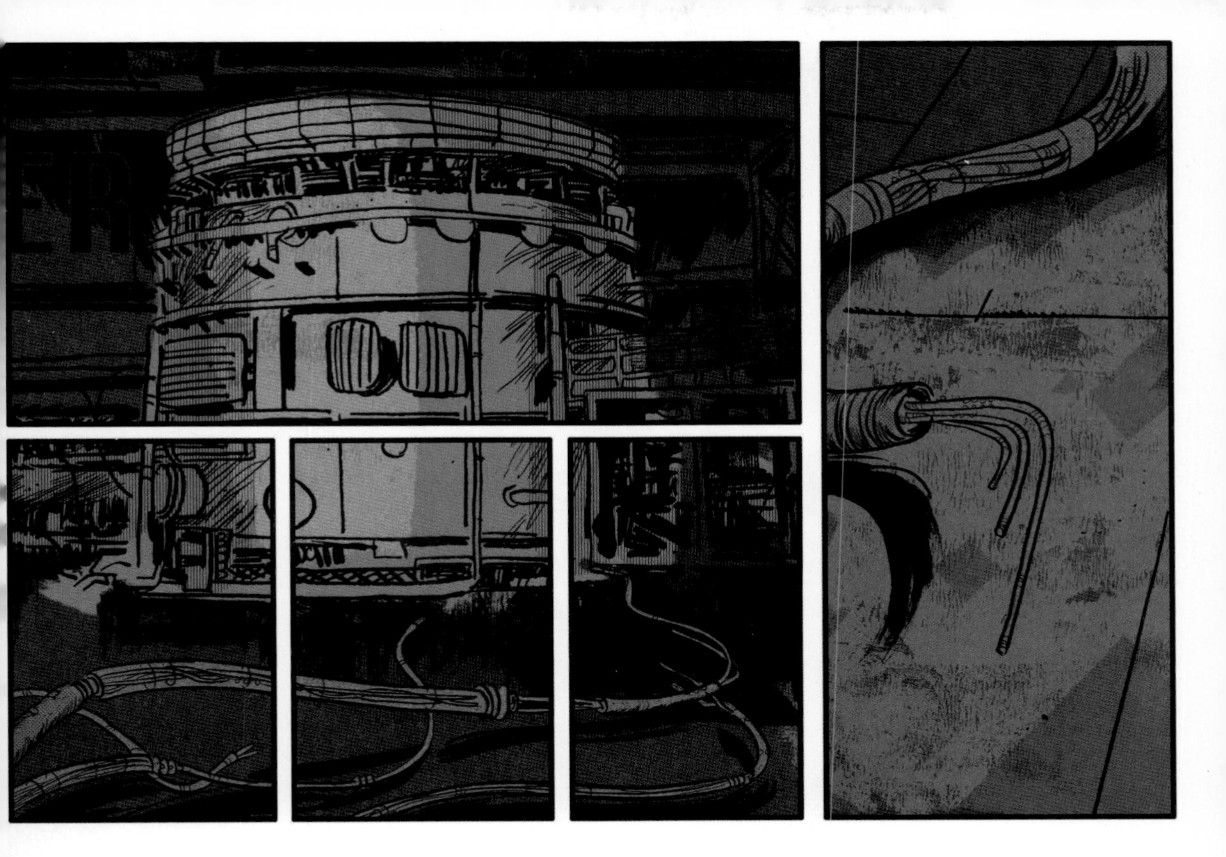

NEW YORK CITY.
HOW DID IT GO WITH THE BIG HAIRY GUY AND THE SKINNY LITTLE NERD?

I ASSUME WELL. LET ME SEE...

HE HAS ALREADY LEFT BIGFOOT'S GROTTO AND CONNECTED WITH MR. BLUESKY.
AHEAD OF SCHEDULE! I LIKE...
WAIT A MINUTE, YOU'RE READIN' THE TEA LEAVES?

YOU'RE A FUCKING **WITCH!**

AFTER ALL YOU HAVE SEEN, **TEA LEAVES** CONNECTED THE DOTS?
YOUR INNOCENCE IS PRECIOUS, BUT HONEY, I AM **NOT** "A FUCKING WITCH."

I AM **THE** FUCKING WITCH.

WELL, ARE YOU A GOOD WITCH?

DETECTIVE CASE, THERE IS NO SUCH THING AS A GOOD WITCH.

NOW LISTEN TO ME, JOHN. I'M GOING TO READ YOUR PALM.

YOU HAVE AN INTERESTING LIFELINE HERE.
BUT LIKE EVERYONE ELSE'S, IT ENDS ABRUPTLY. TONIGHT.

YOU NEED TO KNOW THAT EVERY TIME WE HAVE DONE THIS, I'VE HAD TO PERFORM A RITUAL.
EACH TIME, THE PERSON IN *YOUR* POSITION HAS BEEN A VARIABLE. BINDER, ME, LADY IRONWRATH HERE, SOME OTHERS... WE HAVE ALL BEEN HERE BEFORE. YOU HAVE NOT.
IT IS ALWAYS A GOOD PERSON WHO IS ASKED TO MAKE A TERRIBLE ***SACRIFICE***.

PLEASE, JOHN COME WITH US.

ABOVE THE PENTAGON...

BLOOP!

CRAP. I NEED TO FEED MY CAT.

THEY'RE OBLIGATE CARNIVORES, YOU KNOW? HE COULD STARVE.
I UNDERSTAND HOW YOU FEEL. WHEN I CONTRACTED FOR THIS JOB, I LEFT WHAT YOU MIGHT CONSIDER A PET BACK AT HOME. YOU WOULD FIND ITS SMELL AND APPEARANCE ALARMING. BUT...
...I MISS HIM, IN A MANNER OF SPEAKING.

I HAVE TO DIE TODAY, DON'T I?

YES. WE ALL DIE TODAY. THAT IS WHY I'VE BEEN SO WELL PAID--IT IS A SUICIDE RUN.
THAT IS UNLESS THERE IS A MIRACLE AND YOU CAN STOP **BABEL**.
IN WHICH CASE, ***YOU*** WILL STILL DIE, BUT SOME MAY LIVE. PERHAPS EVEN YOUR CAT...

NOBODY KNOWS ME WELL ENOUGH TO KNOW TO FEED MY CAT. I KILLED MY ONLY FRIEND YESTERDAY.
FUCK.

BENEATH THE SHIP...

OUTSIDE THE SHIP...

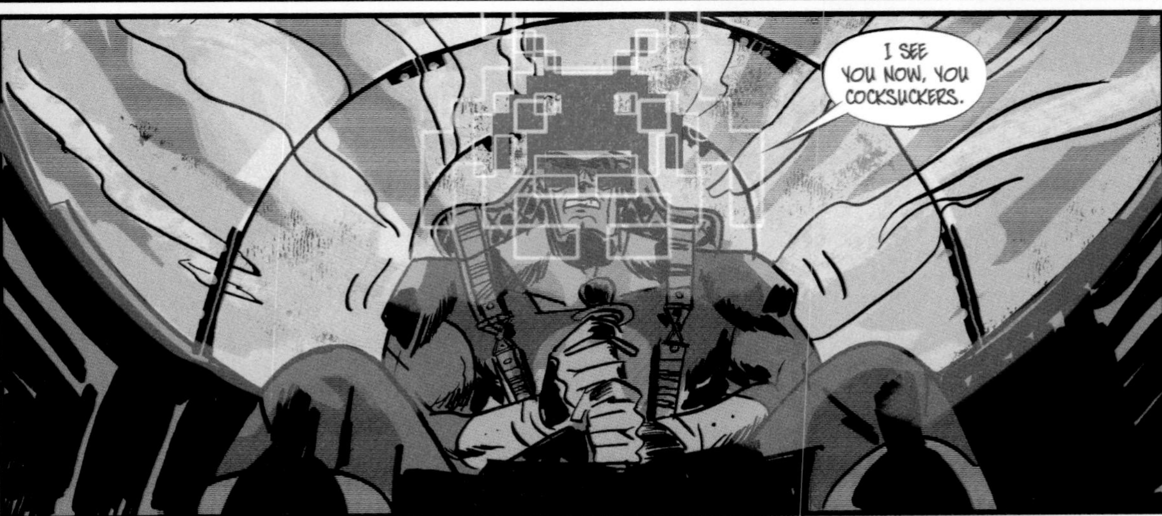
I SEE YOU NOW, YOU COCKSUCKERS.

THIS IS A DAY ABOUT **CHOICES,** JOHN.
YOU THINK I DON'T SEE THAT PIG STICKER YOU GOT HIDIN' BEHIND YOUR BACK?!
WHAT'S THAT GOT TO DO WITH **CHOICE?** YOU'RE PLANNING TO SACRIFICE MY ASS RIGHT HERE ON THIS ALTAR!

I DO APOLOGIZE. I JUST DON'T KNOW HOW TO CARRY IT WITHOUT MAKING YOU NERVOUS.
YOU MAKING ME EVEN MORE NERVOUS WITH THIS SNEAKY SHIT.

OFTEN WHEN WE EXPLAIN THE GRAVITY OF THE PERILOUS SITUATION THAT THE WORLD PRESENTLY FINDS ITSELF IN, THE RANDOM INNOCENT REJECTS HIS OR HER ROLE IN THIS WHOLE MESS. SO WE MUST...
...PERSUADE THEM.
THIS IS THE HARDEST PART OF THE JOB--WE HAVE TO CONVINCE A NORMAL PERSON THAT THEY HAVE TO TAKE A KNIFE TO THE HEART IF THEY WANT TO SAVE THE WORLD.

SO YOU ARE PLANNING TO HUMAN SACRIFICE ME? THE FUCK YOU MEAN, "NORMAL PERSON," WITCH?

PLEASE, JOHN. HEAR HER OUT.
WHAT IS THERE TO HEAR? YOU WANT ME TO DIE SO YOU ALL CAN LIVE!?

WE ALL DIE ANYWAY. AT LEAST WITH YOUR SACRIFICE WE HAVE A CHANCE TO SURVIVE IN ANOTHER TIMELINE. WE CAN TRY AGAIN. A NEW PLAN!
IF YOU DO NOT ALLOW THE SACRIFICE, THE ENERGY RELEASED WILL RIP THE EARTH IN TWO AND WE WILL BE NO MORE.

HOW THE HELL DO YOU KNOW THAT?
I'VE SEEN WHAT THAT KID CAN DO. HE'S TOUGH AS NAILS AND HE'S GOT THAT DEMON ON HIS SIDE. MAYBE HE CAN BEAT THE **WHATEVER IT IS** YOU'RE SO SCARED OF.

HOW DO I KNOW? BECAUSE SAVING THIS PLANET HAS BEEN LIKE PICKING AN IMPOSSIBLE LOCK, AND I HAVE BEEN AT IT LONGER THAN I CAN REMEMBER.
NO MATTER WHAT COMBINATION WE USE, NO MATTER HOW MANY HUMAN VARIABLES WE MANIPULATE, WE NEVER WIN.

WHAT DOES THAT MEAN? NEVER WIN?

WE HAVE FAILED NINE TIMES.
EACH TIME, AN **INNOCENT** HAD TO DIE IN ORDER TO COMPLETE A RITUAL THAT TAKES FIVE MONTHS TO PREPARE.

SO WHAT? YOU HIT THE RESET BUTTON? ALL I HAVE TO DO IS LET YOU KILL ME?

YES, THAT'S RIGHT. DEPENDING ON THE **QUALITY** OF THE SACRIFICE, WE CAN GO BACK FURTHER IN TIME BY MOVING OVER TO ONE OF AN **INFINITE** NUMBER OF TIMELINES.
ONCE WE'RE THERE, YOU'LL HAVE THE CHANCE TO LIVE AGAIN. IT'S THE BEST WE CAN DO UNTIL WE FIND A TIMELINE THAT WE CAN **WIN** IN.
MAYBE WE CAN MAKE A DEAL.

BE CAREFUL, LADY IRONWRATH. DO NOT MAKE PROMISES THAT WE CANNOT KEEP. DOING SUCH THINGS COULD JEOPARDIZE THE PRIMARY OBJECTIVE.
WHAT DO YOU MEAN? LIKE MAYBE NEXT TIME YOU CAN WARN ME ABOUT 9-11?
OR STOP WHAT HAPPENED TO THE STATION LAST NIGHT?

MEANWHILE, ABOVE THE PENTAGON.
FIRING!

FUCK YEAH! **AMERICA!** WOOOO!

JESUS CHRIST!
HARDLY.

YEEEEEEE-HAW!

KA-BAAAM

HE JUST FLEW RIGHT INTO US! THAT IDIOT JUST COMMITTED SUICIDE!
YES, AND NOW WE'RE EXPOSED. IT'S TIME. SUPER-THERMITE HAS NEVER BEEN THIS TENACIOUS OR IDEALISTIC BEFORE. THIS IS NOT A GOOD SIGN! BABEL KNOWS WE ARE HERE.

TIME?! ALREADY?
DOWN THERE, A MONSTER IS MARSHALING ITS FORCES.
IN MINUTES, HIS BETTER HALF, THE CRAFT ITSELF, WILL BE READY TO DRAW UP THE ENERGY FROM THE IMMINENT EXPLOSION. THIS TIME WE THINK IT IS ITER.

EATER?

THE INTERNATIONAL THERMONUCLEAR EXPERIMENTAL REACTOR. ITER.

I DON'T GET ANY OF THIS BUT THAT SOUNDS BAD.
IT IS, BUT THAT THING THAT LIVES INSIDE YOU--

MERRY SUE?

YES. MERRY SUE IS AN ANCIENT THING, AN ARCHON--PART OF THE ORIGINAL FOUNDATIONS OF THE SENTIENT EARTH. THERE IS ENOUGH POWER THERE TO STOP HIM, BUT IT'S NOT LIKELY. STILL, WE MUST TRY.
IN A MOMENT YOU WILL DROP FROM THE BELLY OF THIS VESSEL. AT THE SAME TIME WE WILL LAUNCH A PHOTON TORPEDO AT THE TARGET. YOU WILL DROP INTO THE RESULTING OPENING AND CONFRONT THE TARGET.
YOU SAID "DROP" TWICE. HOW?

OF COURSE.

THIS SUCKS.
I KNOW, YOUNG MAN. LIFE'S A BITCH, EH?

PROMISE ME YOU'LL WARN ME ABOUT 9-11. PROMISE ME YOU'LL MAKE ME AND MY PARTNER BELIEVE.
SAL RAN RIGHT INTO THE TRADE CENTER THAT DAY. NEVER FORGAVE MYSELF FOR FREEZING LIKE I DID.
WARNING EITHER OF YOU WILL POTENTIALLY DERAIL OUR NEXT ATTEMPT BEFORE IT EVEN HAS A CHANCE TO BEGIN.
MIGHT AS WELL SEE WHAT HAPPENS, ALEXANDRA.
WHY NOT? NOTHING ELSE HAS WORKED.

IF YOU ALL DON'T PROMISE, I AIN'T GOING TO LET YOU DO THIS TO ME.
I GOT TO AT LEAST KEEP SAL FROM GOING IN THERE, OKAY? THAT'S THE DEAL.

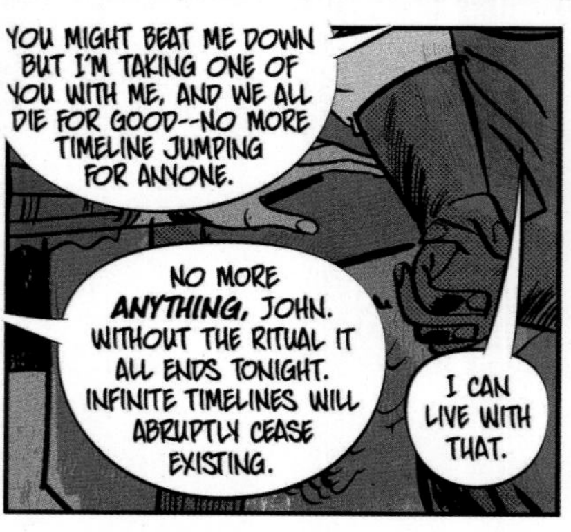
YOU MIGHT BEAT ME DOWN BUT I'M TAKING ONE OF YOU WITH ME, AND WE ALL DIE FOR GOOD--NO MORE TIMELINE JUMPING FOR ANYONE.
NO MORE **ANYTHING,** JOHN. WITHOUT THE RITUAL IT ALL ENDS TONIGHT. INFINITE TIMELINES WILL ABRUPTLY CEASE EXISTING.
I CAN LIVE WITH THAT.

IT WAS NICE TO MEET YOU, MR. BLUESKY.
WE WILL SEE EACH OTHER AGAIN, BRANDON.
BE BRAVE.
WE WILL GUIDE YOU DOWN WITH A TRACTOR BEAM AND THEN PULVERIZE THE LAYERS WITH BLASTS TO PENETRATE THE SURFACE.
WAIT--

FUUUUUUUCK THIS!

COMMAND, I JUST SPOTTED A MAN FALLING FROM THE CRAFT!
MAINTAIN FOCUSED ATTACK, JUGHEAD. WE DON'T HAVE TIME TO WORRY ABOUT DEAD, OR SOON-TO-BE-DEAD, MEN.

OH SHIT! IT HURTS!

FIRE.
BOOM
BOOM

KA-BOOM

UNF!

NOW WHAT?
THEY SENT THE DEMON BINDER. I DID TRY TO REMOVE YOU FROM THE BOARD. YOU'RE A PEST.
I SUPPOSE YOU'RE WHAT THEY'RE CALLING "BABEL." AREN'T YOU A BIT COLLOQUIAL FOR A SPACE MONSTER?
WHY DO YOU THINK THEY CALL ME THAT? I GAVE YOU LANGUAGE. I AM YOUR CREATOR, AFTER ALL.
YOU? CREATOR OF WHAT?
YOU! I SUPPOSE YOU DESERVE AN EXPLANATION BEFORE YOU DIE: HUMANS ONLY EXIST TO FULFILL THE SINGULAR PURPOSE THAT I HAVE DESIGNED THEM FOR: SLAVERY.

"UNDERSTAND: I WAS STRANDED IN THIS SOLAR SYSTEM OVER 75,000 YEARS AGO. A MERE MOMENT IN MY NIGH ETERNAL LIFETIME."

I AM YOUR GOD. I CREATED YOU TO MAKE THE DEVICE THAT I WILL USE TO TEAR THE EARTH ASUNDER--AND NOW THAT MEN HAVE FULFILLED THEIR PURPOSE, I WILL EXTINGUISH YOUR LIFE.
OH, HOLY SHIT! LET GO!

NOW IT'S TIME FOR YOU AND YOUR LITTLE PARASITE TO **DIE**.

KRIKKLL RIKKKR
KRKKKKR
RKRK
L-RKK

ARRRGH!

OH MAN...

I CANNOT DO THIS. I WILL NOT MAKE THIS PROMISE.

WHAT?! YOU CAN'T BE SERIOUS, ALEXANDRA! DO IT!

YOU DO IT THEN!
NO! I'M NOT THE WITCH. YOU ARE. I DON'T KNOW THE FUCKING SPELL!

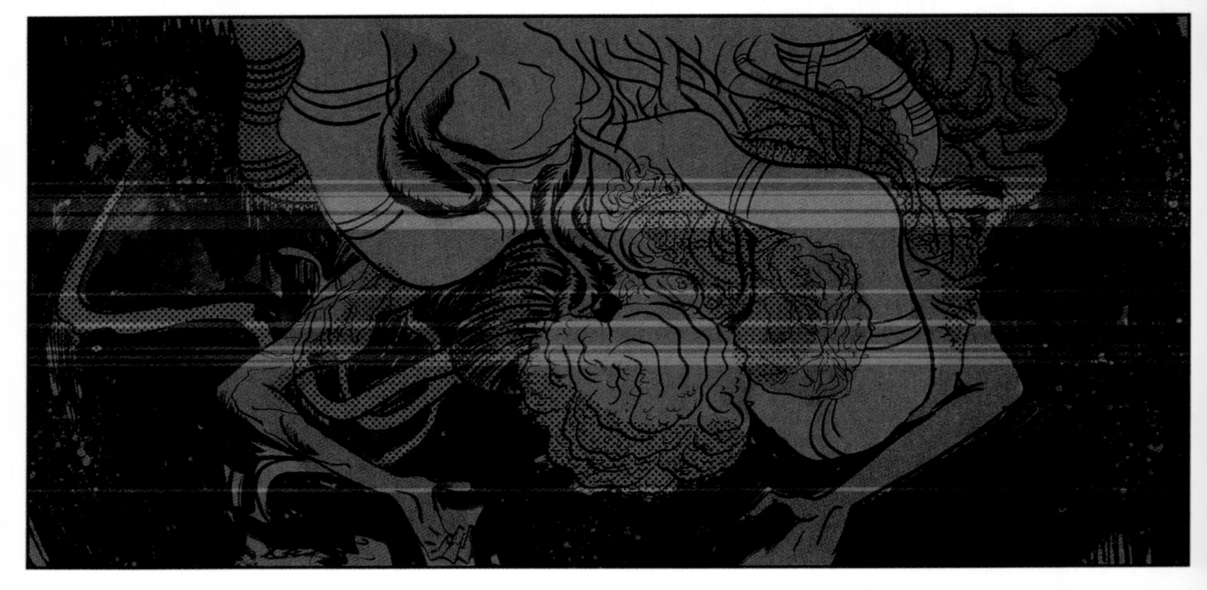

MRA-OAR!

IT'S NOT GOING TO BE THAT EASY!

DIE, YOU UGLY MOTHERFUCKER! DIE!

SKAT

BREAK!

BREAK, GOD DAMN YOU!
FOOL! I AM YOUR GOD AND YOU ARE ALREADY WAY TOO LATE!

SSSSKKKAAA

KRAA

KRA KOOM

I FUCKING KILLED IT, BUT IT'S TOO LATE.
IF YOU CAN HEAR ME, WITCH: IT'S OVER. MERRY SUE IS TELLING ME WE'VE FAILED AGAIN.

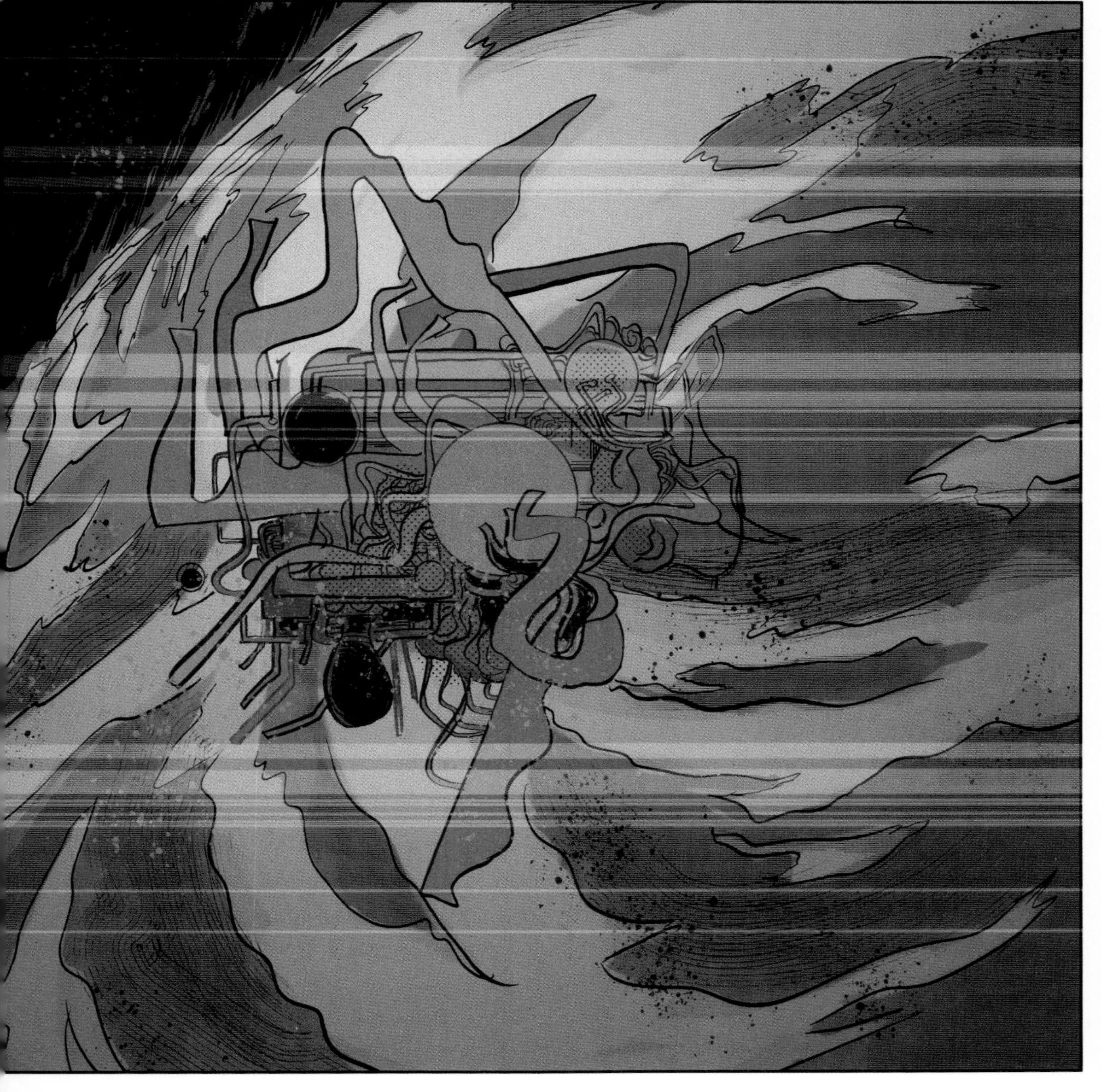

HE FAILED. **THEY** FAILED. IN MINUTES, THE PLANET WILL RIP IN HALF...

KNOW WHAT? I'M ***TIRED*** OF THIS SHIT.

DON'T YOU DO THIS, ALEXANDRA DAVID-NEEL! DON'T YOU ***DARE*** LIE DOWN AND DIE!
HEY, YA'LL NEED TO QUIT FIGHTING. GIVE ME THAT.

DON'T YOU GO ***GOOD WITCH*** ON ME, LADY! YOU GOT A ***PROMISE*** TO KEEP.

A PERFECT SACRIFICE.
UTTERLY SELFLESS...

NOT TRUE. I'M SAVING MY SOUL.
UURRK

WHEN YOU FIND US...
YOU TELL SAL... I RAN *TOWARD* THE DANGER THIS TIME.

I WILL HOLD HER TO IT, JOHN.

I HOPE I SEE YOU AGAIN, IRONWRATH.

AND AS INNOCENT BLOOD STICKS TO THE SANDS OF TIME, GREAT GODDESS I **BESEECH** THEE TO LIFT UP THE HOURGLASS AND DASH IT UPON THE FIRMAMENT!

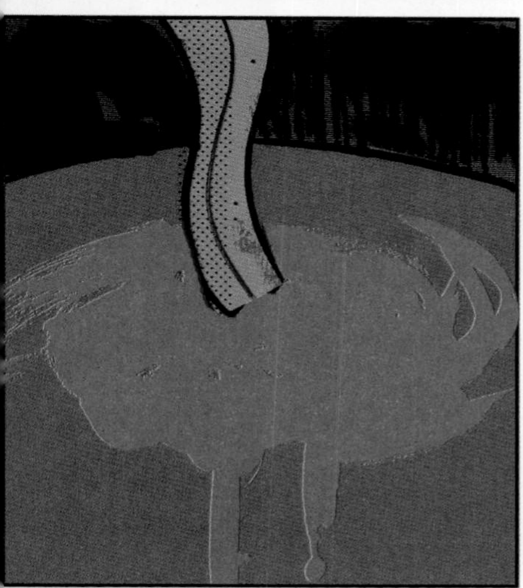

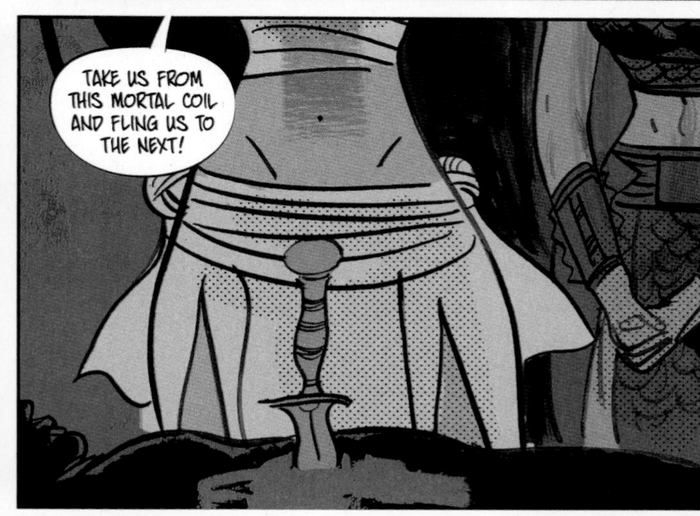
TAKE US FROM THIS MORTAL COIL AND FLING US TO THE NEXT!

"SO MOTE IT BE!"

JUDGING BY MY LUDICROUSLY LARGE *TITS* AND ALL OF THE *POUCHES* YOU HAVE ON YOUR, *AHEM,* *"COSTUME"*--I WOULD SAY...

...IT LOOKS LIKE WE'RE IN THE LATE 90s, MAYBE EARLY 2000s.

ART BY
DAN FRAGA

ART BY
DONAL DeLAY
DONAL

JUDGEMENT
THE TOWER
THE
DEATH.
ACE OF CUPS
ART BY
ROBERT SCHNIEDERS

ART BY
ROBERT SCHNIEDERS